#2

MY BOYFRIEND IS A MONSTER

Made for Each Other

OR

I MADE MY PROM DATE

OR

HUNKENSTEIN

OR

LOVE IN STITCHES

OR

OUR LOVE'S ALIIIIIIVE!!

PAUL D. STORRIE

Illustrated by ELDON COWGUR

GRAPHIC UNIVERSE™ · MINNEAPOLIS · NEW YORK

STORY BY
PAUL D. STORRIE

ART, LETTERING,
AND COVER BY
ELDON COWGUR

Graphic Universe™
A division of Lerner Publishing Group, Inc.
241 First Avenue North
Minneapolis, MN 55401 U.S.A.

Website address: www.lernerbooks.com

Library of Congress Cataloging-in-Publication Data

Storrie, Paul D.
    Made for each other / by Paul D. Storrie ; illustrated by Eldon Cowgur.
      p.   cm. — (My boyfriend is a monster ; #2)
    Summary: High school students Maria and Tom are immediately attracted to each other, but an envious monster named Hedy will stop at nothing to destroy their romance.
    ISBN: 978-0-7613-5601-1 (lib. bdg. : alk. paper)
    1. Graphic novels. [1. Graphic novels. 2. Horror stories. 3. Monsters—Fiction. 4. High schools—Fiction. 5. Schools—Fiction.] I. Cowgur, Eldon, ill. II. Title.
PZ7.7.S756Mb 2011
741.5'973—dc22   2010028722

Manufactured in the United States of America
1 – DP – 12/31/10

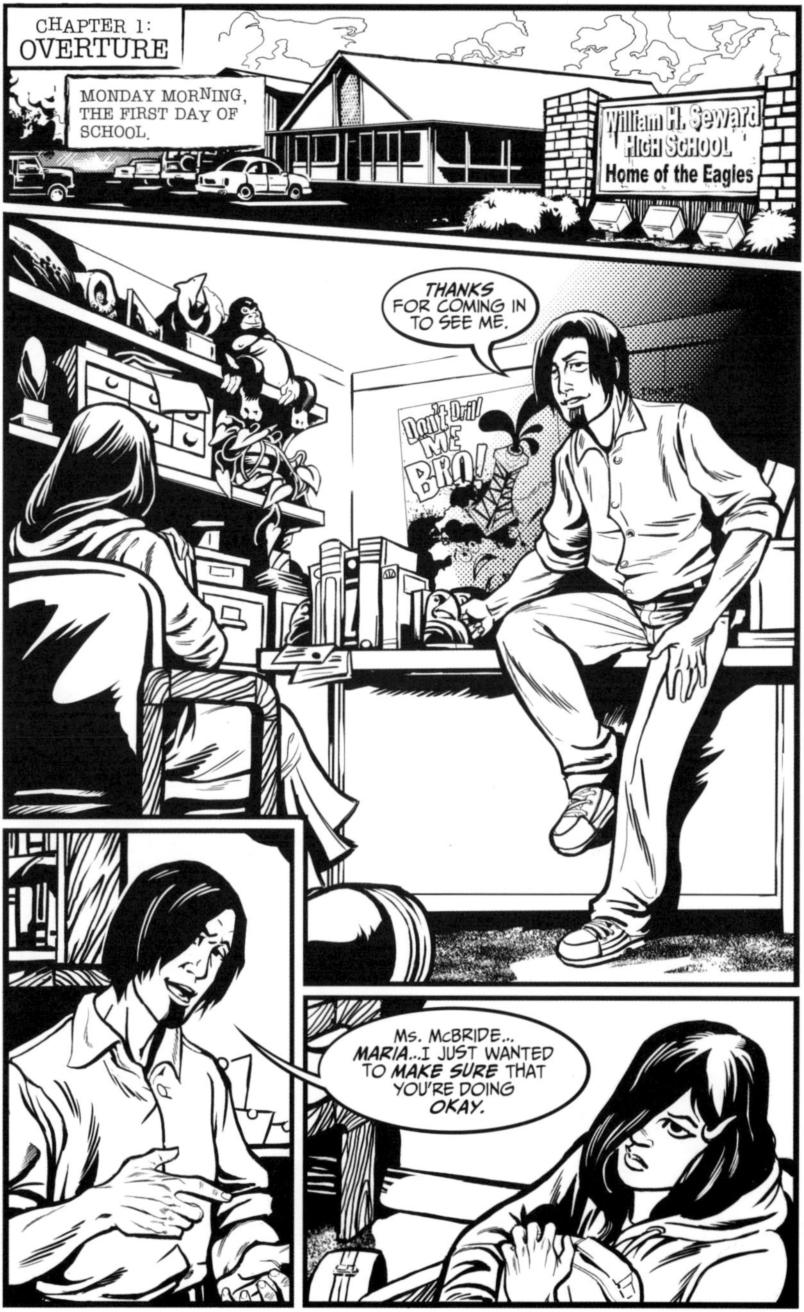
CHAPTER 1:
OVERTURE
MONDAY MORNING, THE FIRST DAY OF SCHOOL.
William H. Seward High School
Home of the Eagles
THANKS FOR COMING IN TO SEE ME.
Don't Drill ME BRO!
Ms. McBRIDE... MARIA...I JUST WANTED TO MAKE SURE THAT YOU'RE DOING OKAY.

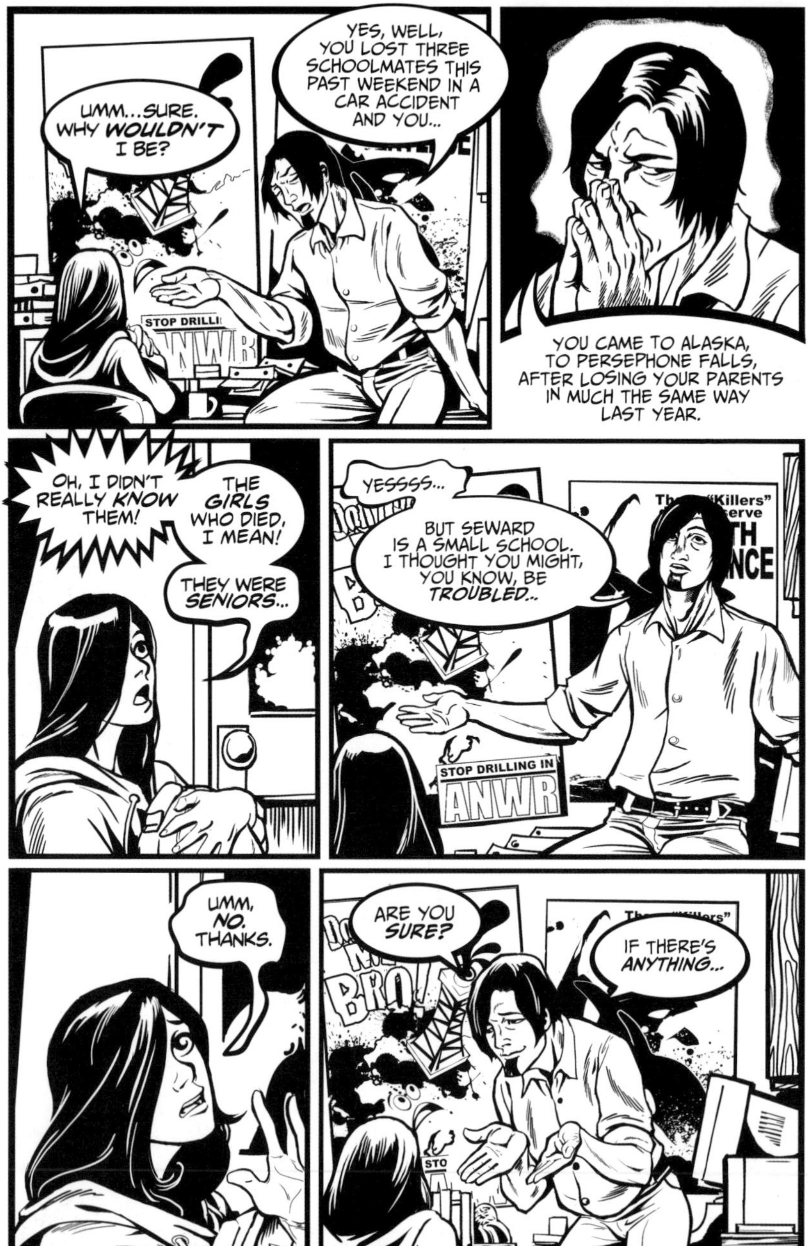
UMM...SURE. WHY *WOULDN'T* I BE?
YES, WELL, YOU LOST THREE SCHOOLMATES THIS PAST WEEKEND IN A CAR ACCIDENT AND YOU...
STOP DRILLI
ANWR
YOU CAME TO ALASKA, TO PERSEPHONE FALLS, AFTER LOSING YOUR PARENTS IN MUCH THE SAME WAY LAST YEAR.
OH, I DIDN'T REALLY *KNOW* THEM!
THE *GIRLS* WHO DIED, I MEAN!
THEY WERE *SENIORS*...
YESSSS...
BUT SEWARD IS A SMALL SCHOOL. I THOUGHT YOU MIGHT, YOU KNOW, BE *TROUBLED*..
STOP DRILLING IN
ANWR
UMM, *NO.* THANKS.
ARE YOU *SURE?*
IF THERE'S *ANYTHING*...

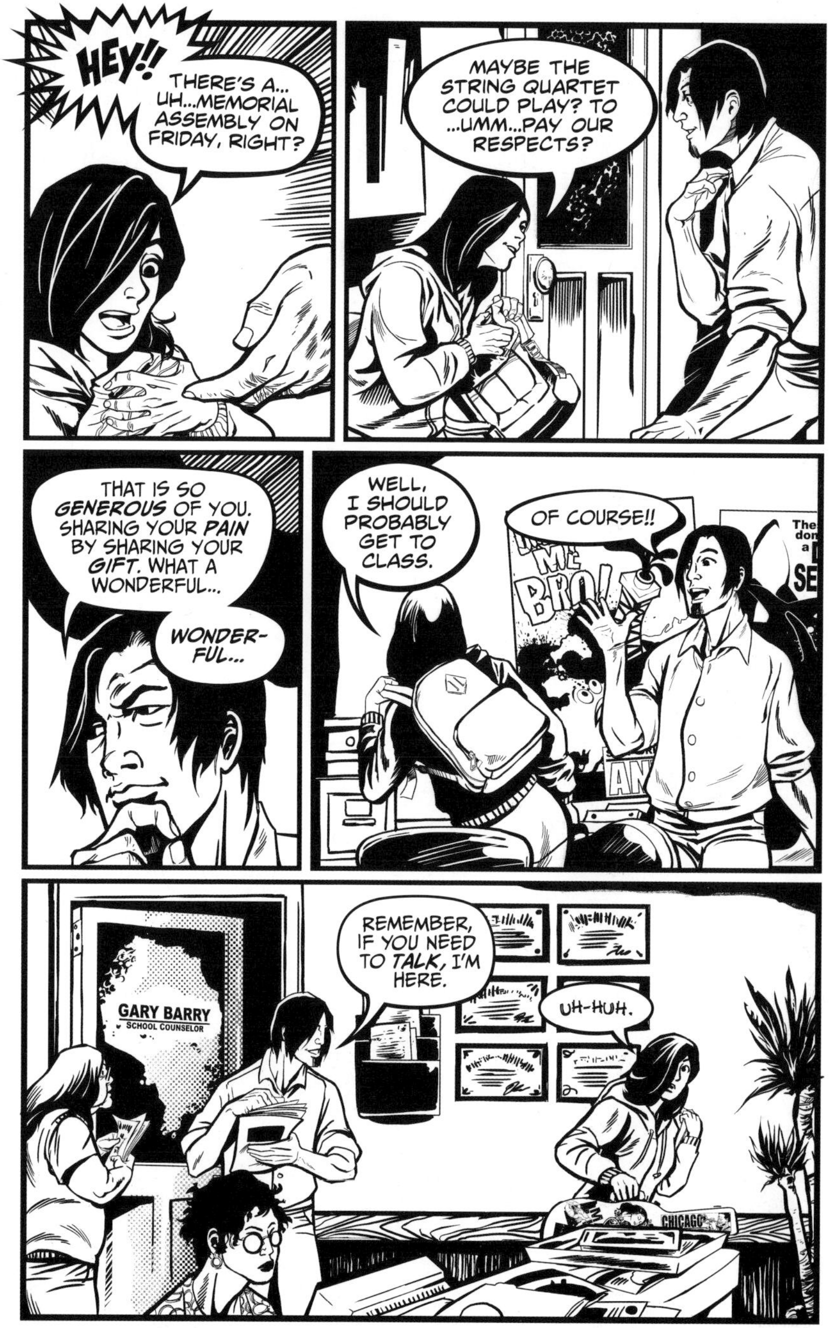
HEY!!
THERE'S A... UH...MEMORIAL ASSEMBLY ON FRIDAY, RIGHT?
MAYBE THE STRING QUARTET COULD PLAY? TO ...UMM...PAY OUR RESPECTS?
THAT IS SO GENEROUS OF YOU. SHARING YOUR PAIN BY SHARING YOUR GIFT. WHAT A WONDERFUL...
WONDER-FUL...
WELL, I SHOULD PROBABLY GET TO CLASS.
OF COURSE!!
REMEMBER, IF YOU NEED TO TALK, I'M HERE.
UH-HUH.
GARY BARRY
SCHOOL COUNSELOR
CHICAGO

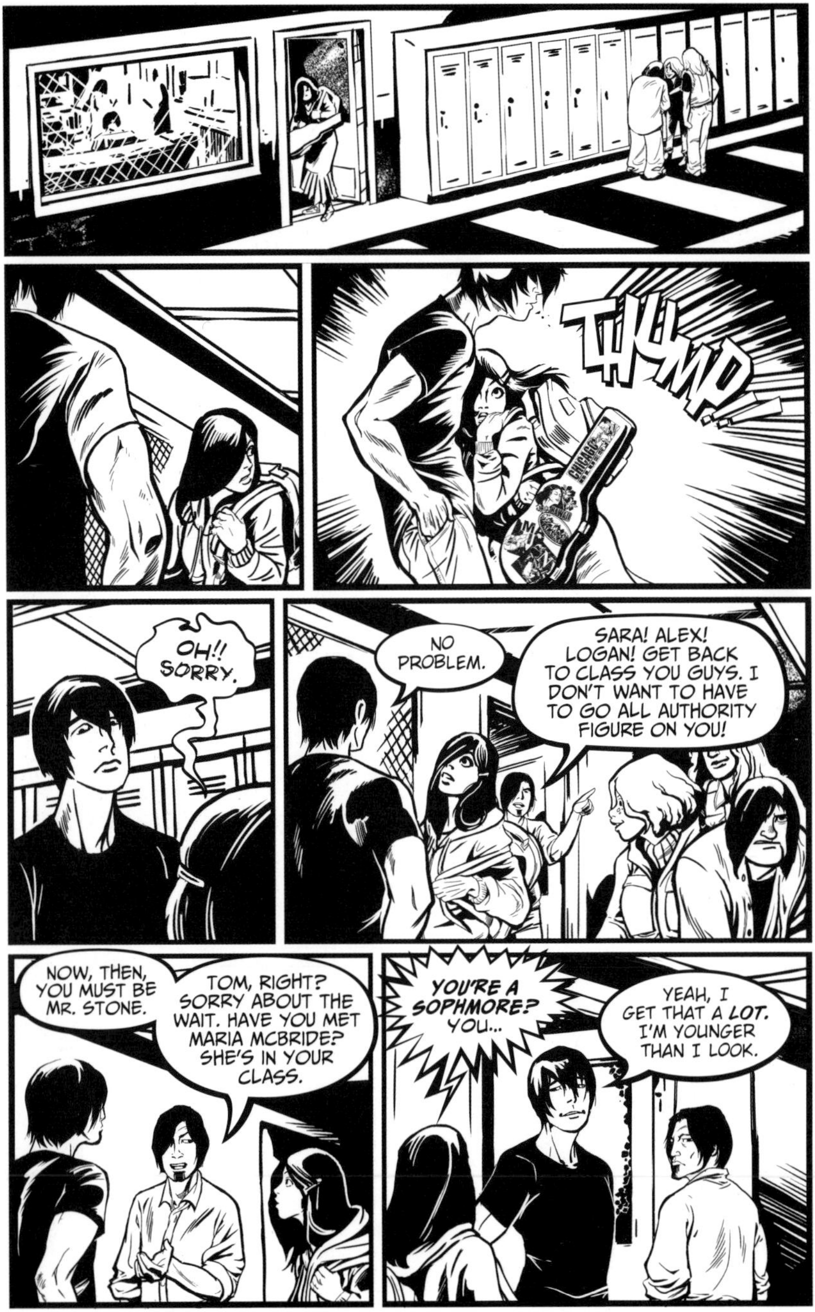
THUMP!!!
OH!! SORRY.
NO PROBLEM.
SARA! ALEX! LOGAN! GET BACK TO CLASS YOU GUYS. I DON'T WANT TO HAVE TO GO ALL AUTHORITY FIGURE ON YOU!
NOW, THEN, YOU MUST BE MR. STONE.
TOM, RIGHT? SORRY ABOUT THE WAIT. HAVE YOU MET MARIA MCBRIDE? SHE'S IN YOUR CLASS.
YOU'RE A SOPHMORE? YOU...
YEAH, I GET THAT A LOT. I'M YOUNGER THAN I LOOK.

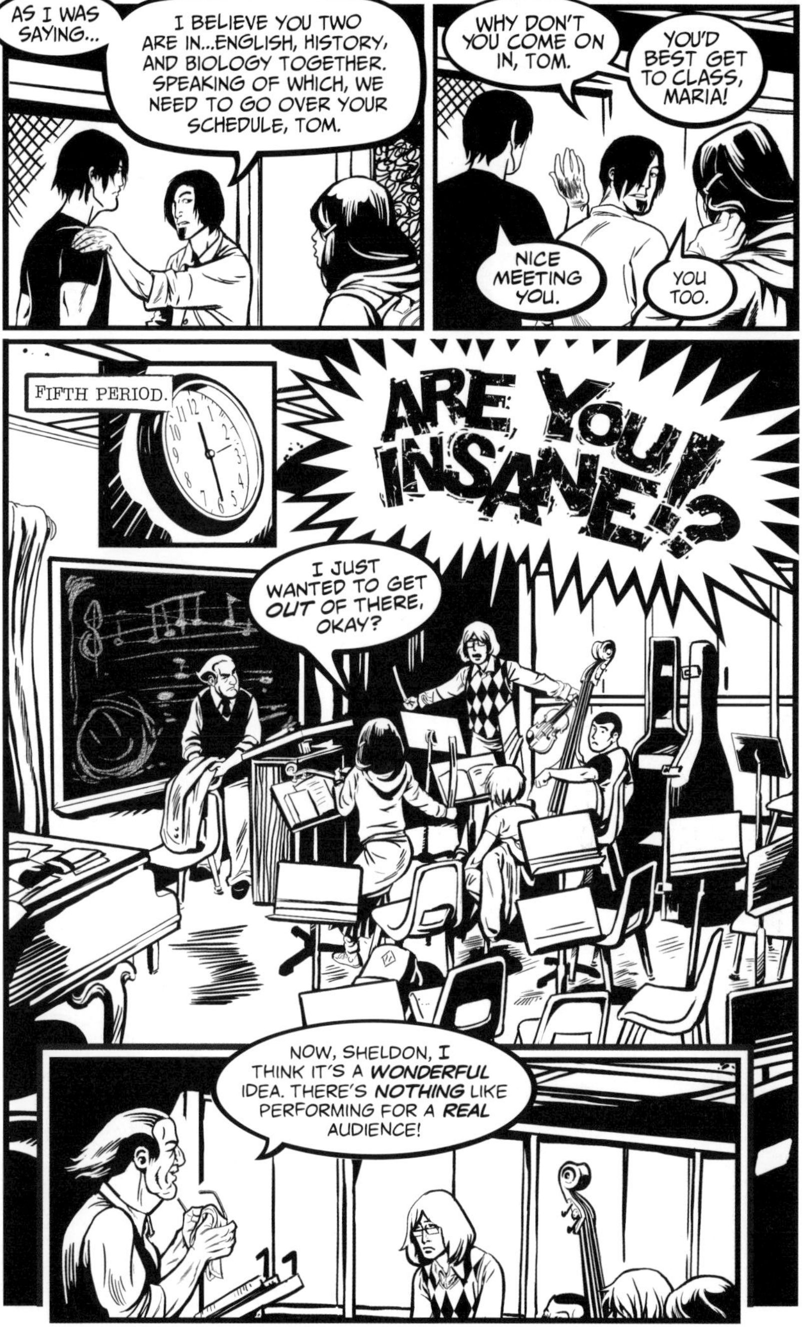
AS I WAS SAYING...
I BELIEVE YOU TWO ARE IN...ENGLISH, HISTORY, AND BIOLOGY TOGETHER. SPEAKING OF WHICH, WE NEED TO GO OVER YOUR SCHEDULE, TOM.
WHY DON'T YOU COME ON IN, TOM.
YOU'D BEST GET TO CLASS, MARIA!
NICE MEETING YOU.
YOU TOO.
FIFTH PERIOD.
ARE YOU INSANE!?
I JUST WANTED TO GET OUT OF THERE, OKAY?
NOW, SHELDON, I THINK IT'S A WONDERFUL IDEA. THERE'S NOTHING LIKE PERFORMING FOR A REAL AUDIENCE!

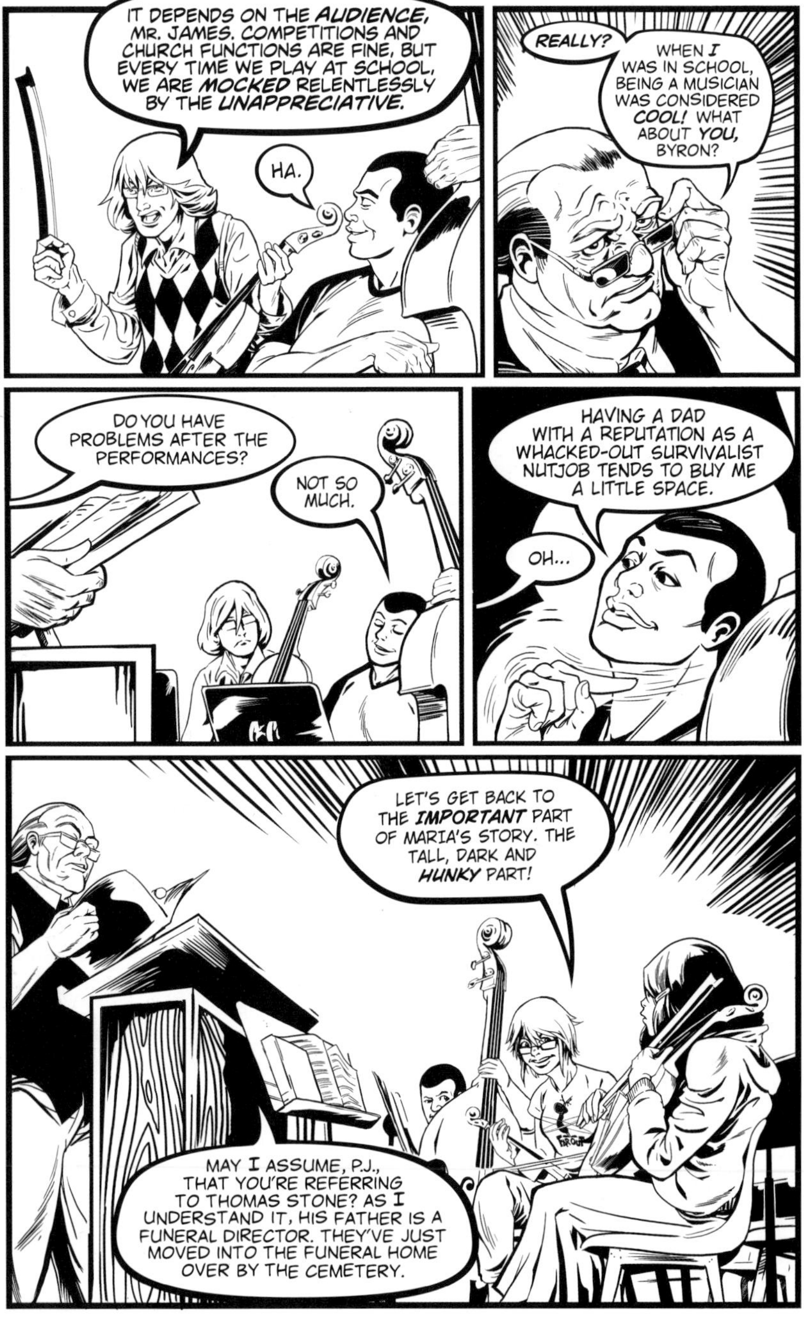
IT DEPENDS ON THE AUDIENCE, MR. JAMES. COMPETITIONS AND CHURCH FUNCTIONS ARE FINE, BUT EVERY TIME WE PLAY AT SCHOOL, WE ARE MOCKED RELENTLESSLY BY THE UNAPPRECIATIVE.
HA.
REALLY?
WHEN I WAS IN SCHOOL, BEING A MUSICIAN WAS CONSIDERED COOL! WHAT ABOUT YOU, BYRON?
DO YOU HAVE PROBLEMS AFTER THE PERFORMANCES?
NOT SO MUCH.
HAVING A DAD WITH A REPUTATION AS A WHACKED-OUT SURVIVALIST NUTJOB TENDS TO BUY ME A LITTLE SPACE.
OH...
LET'S GET BACK TO THE IMPORTANT PART OF MARIA'S STORY. THE TALL, DARK AND HUNKY PART!
MAY I ASSUME, P.J., THAT YOU'RE REFERRING TO THOMAS STONE? AS I UNDERSTAND IT, HIS FATHER IS A FUNERAL DIRECTOR. THEY'VE JUST MOVED INTO THE FUNERAL HOME OVER BY THE CEMETERY.

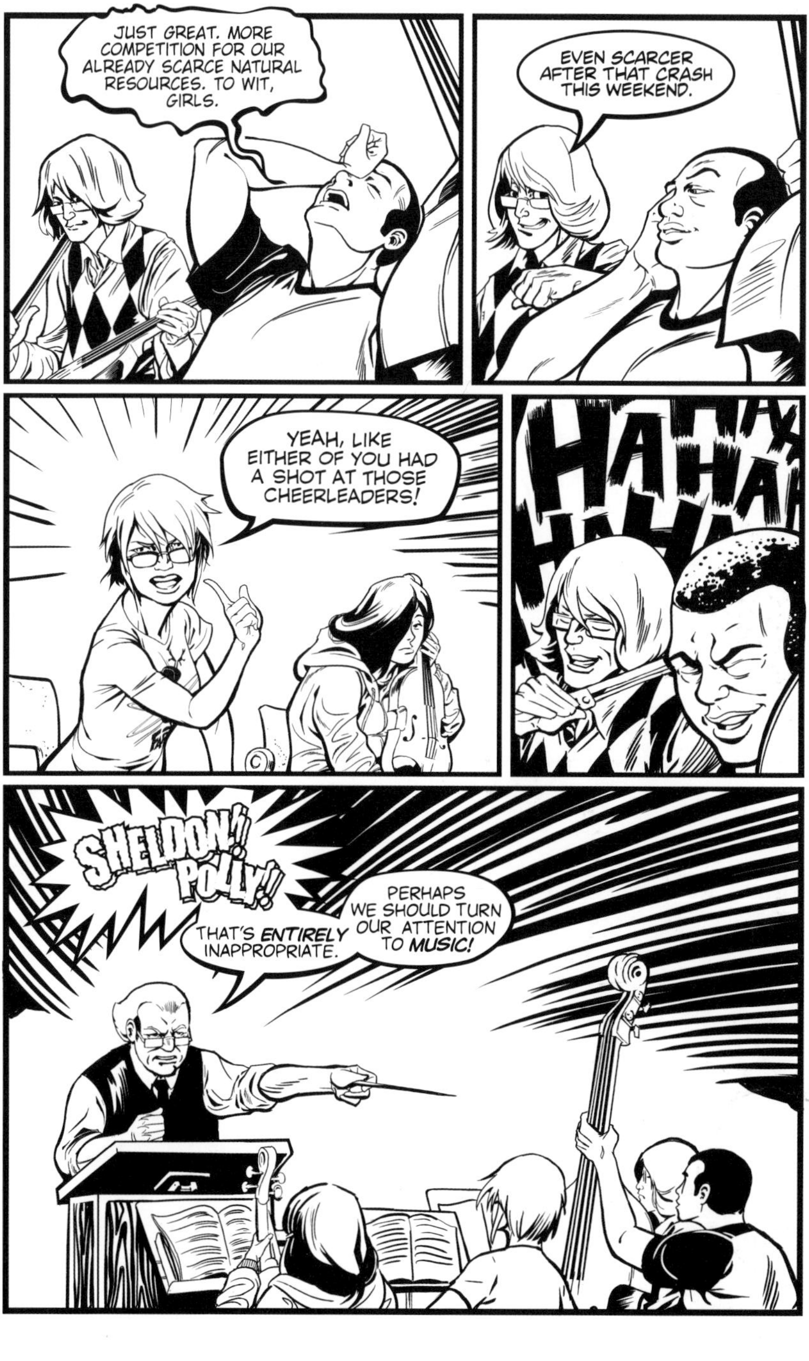
JUST GREAT. MORE COMPETITION FOR OUR ALREADY SCARCE NATURAL RESOURCES. TO WIT, GIRLS.
EVEN SCARCER AFTER THAT CRASH THIS WEEKEND.
YEAH, LIKE EITHER OF YOU HAD A SHOT AT THOSE CHEERLEADERS!
HAHAHAHAHA
SHELDON!! POLLY!!
THAT'S ENTIRELY INAPPROPRIATE.
PERHAPS WE SHOULD TURN OUR ATTENTION TO MUSIC!

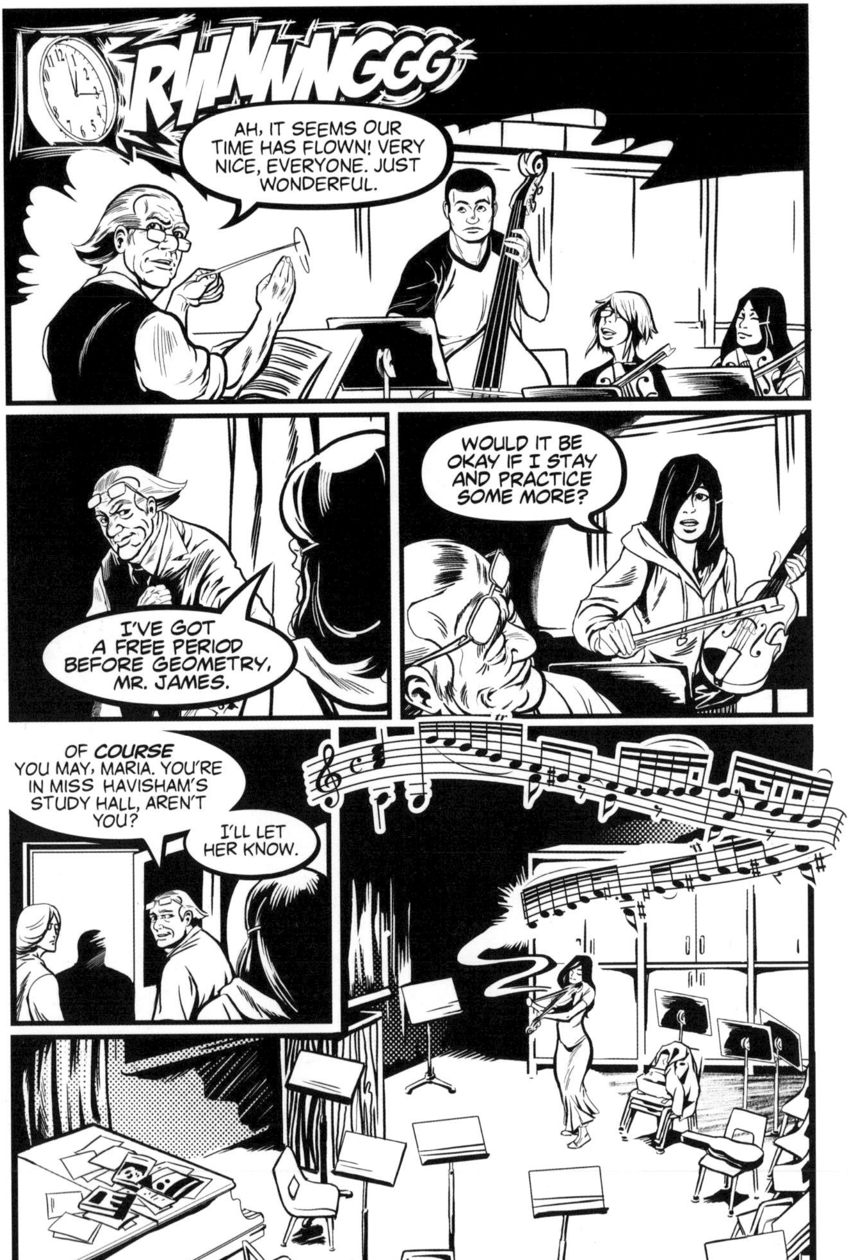
RHNNNNGGG
AH, IT SEEMS OUR TIME HAS FLOWN! VERY NICE, EVERYONE. JUST WONDERFUL.
I'VE GOT A FREE PERIOD BEFORE GEOMETRY, MR. JAMES.
WOULD IT BE OKAY IF I STAY AND PRACTICE SOME MORE?
OF COURSE YOU MAY, MARIA. YOU'RE IN MISS HAVISHAM'S STUDY HALL, AREN'T YOU?
I'LL LET HER KNOW.

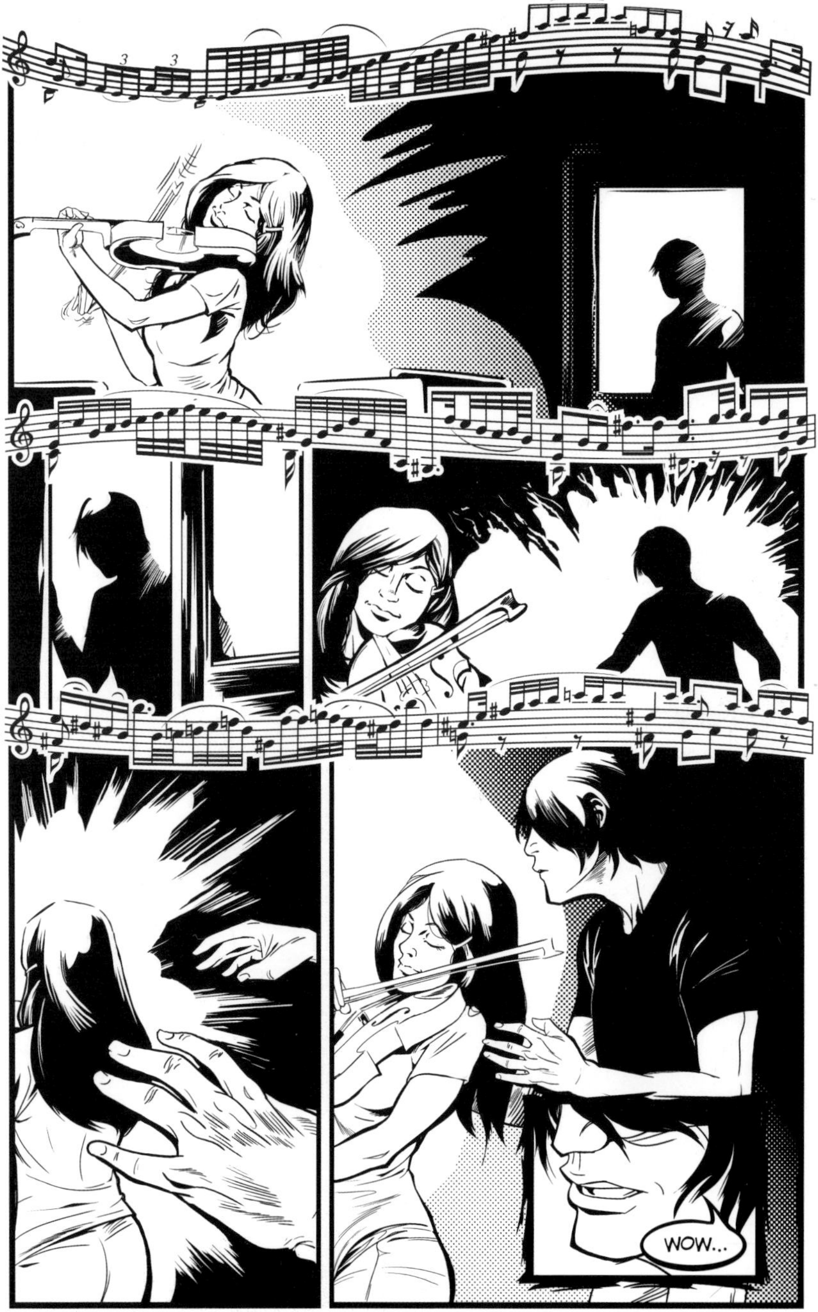
WOW...

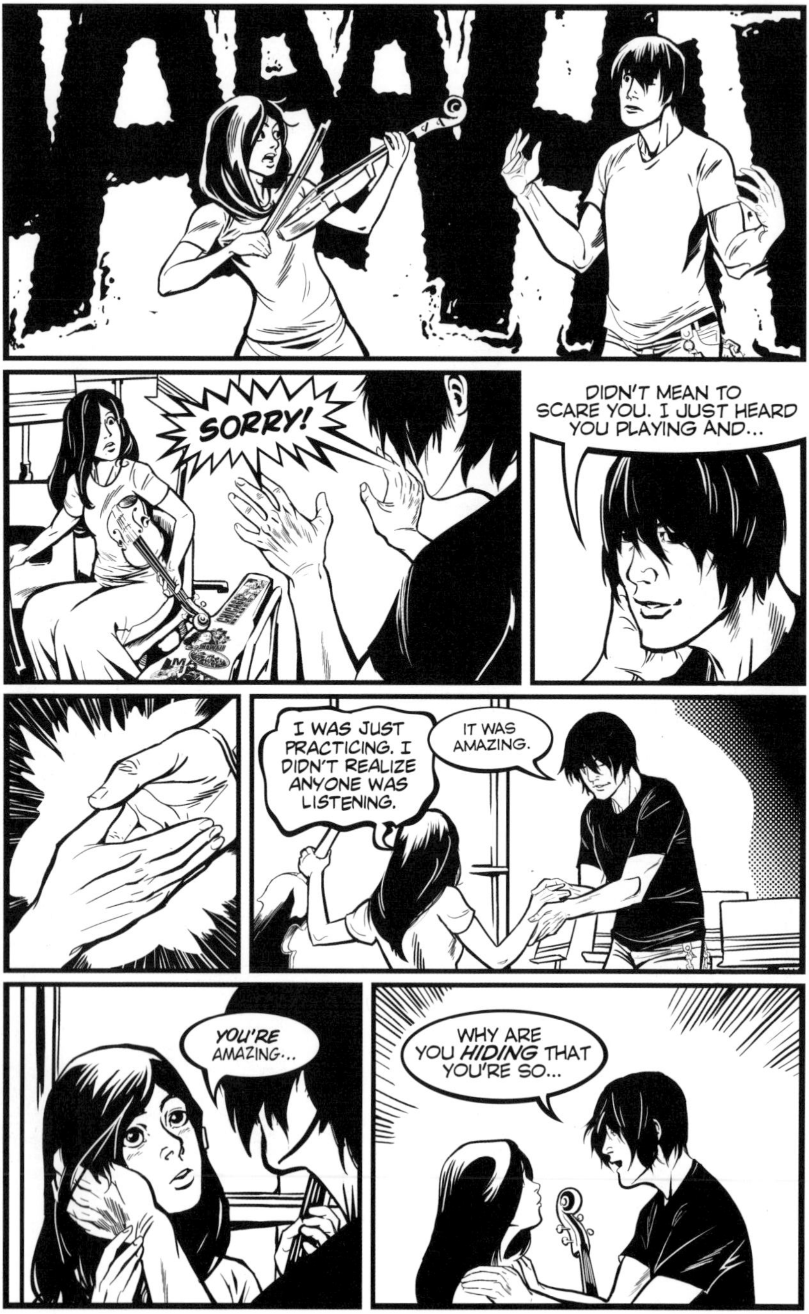
SORRY!
DIDN'T MEAN TO SCARE YOU. I JUST HEARD YOU PLAYING AND...
I WAS JUST PRACTICING. I DIDN'T REALIZE ANYONE WAS LISTENING.
IT WAS AMAZING.
YOU'RE AMAZING...
WHY ARE YOU HIDING THAT YOU'RE SO...

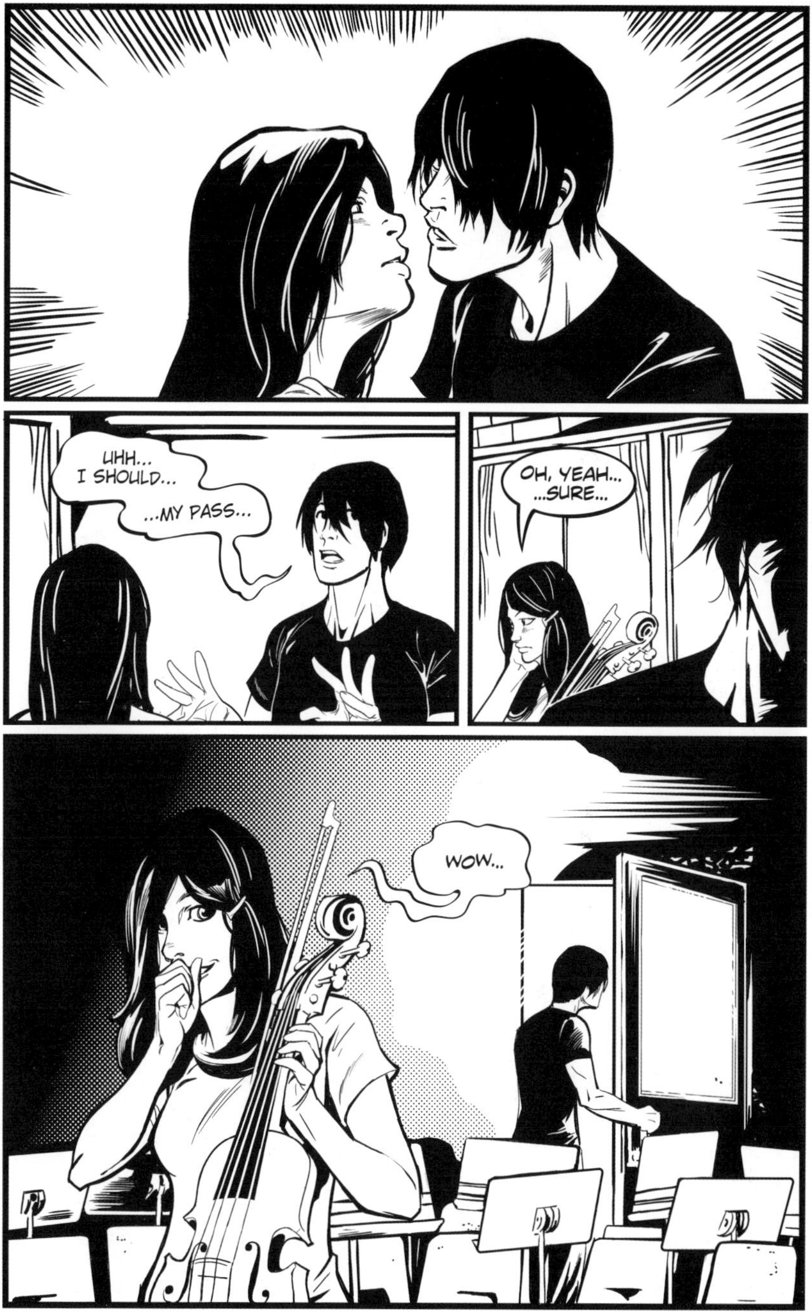
UHH... I SHOULD...
...MY PASS...
OH, YEAH... ...SURE...
WOW...

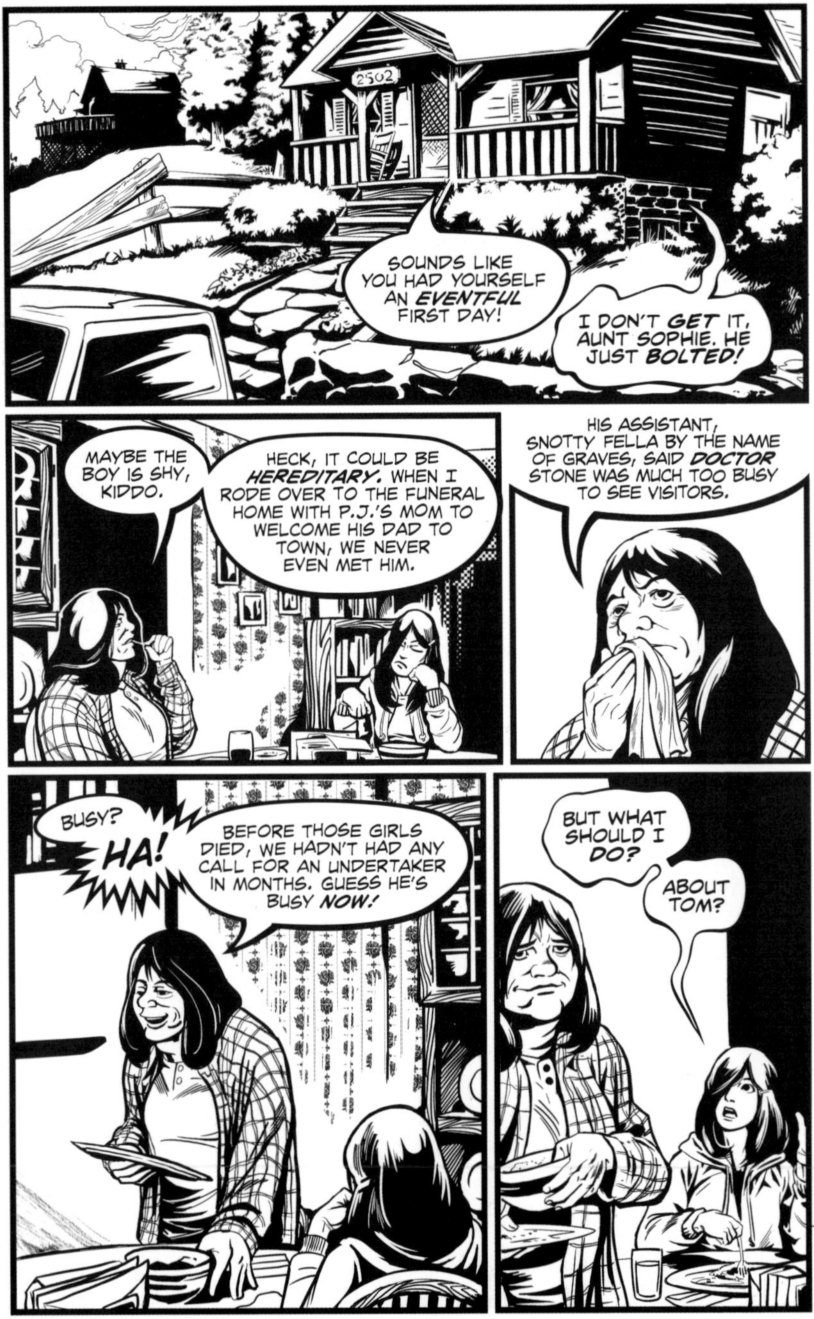
2502
SOUNDS LIKE YOU HAD YOURSELF AN *EVENTFUL* FIRST DAY!
I DON'T *GET* IT, AUNT SOPHIE. HE JUST *BOLTED!*
MAYBE THE BOY IS SHY, KIDDO.
HECK, IT COULD BE *HEREDITARY.* WHEN I RODE OVER TO THE FUNERAL HOME WITH P.J.'S MOM TO WELCOME HIS DAD TO TOWN, WE NEVER EVEN MET HIM.
HIS ASSISTANT, SNOTTY FELLA BY THE NAME OF GRAVES, SAID *DOCTOR* STONE WAS MUCH TOO BUSY TO SEE VISITORS.
BUSY?
HA!
BEFORE THOSE GIRLS DIED, WE HADN'T HAD ANY CALL FOR AN UNDERTAKER IN MONTHS. GUESS HE'S BUSY *NOW!*
BUT WHAT SHOULD I *DO?*
ABOUT TOM?

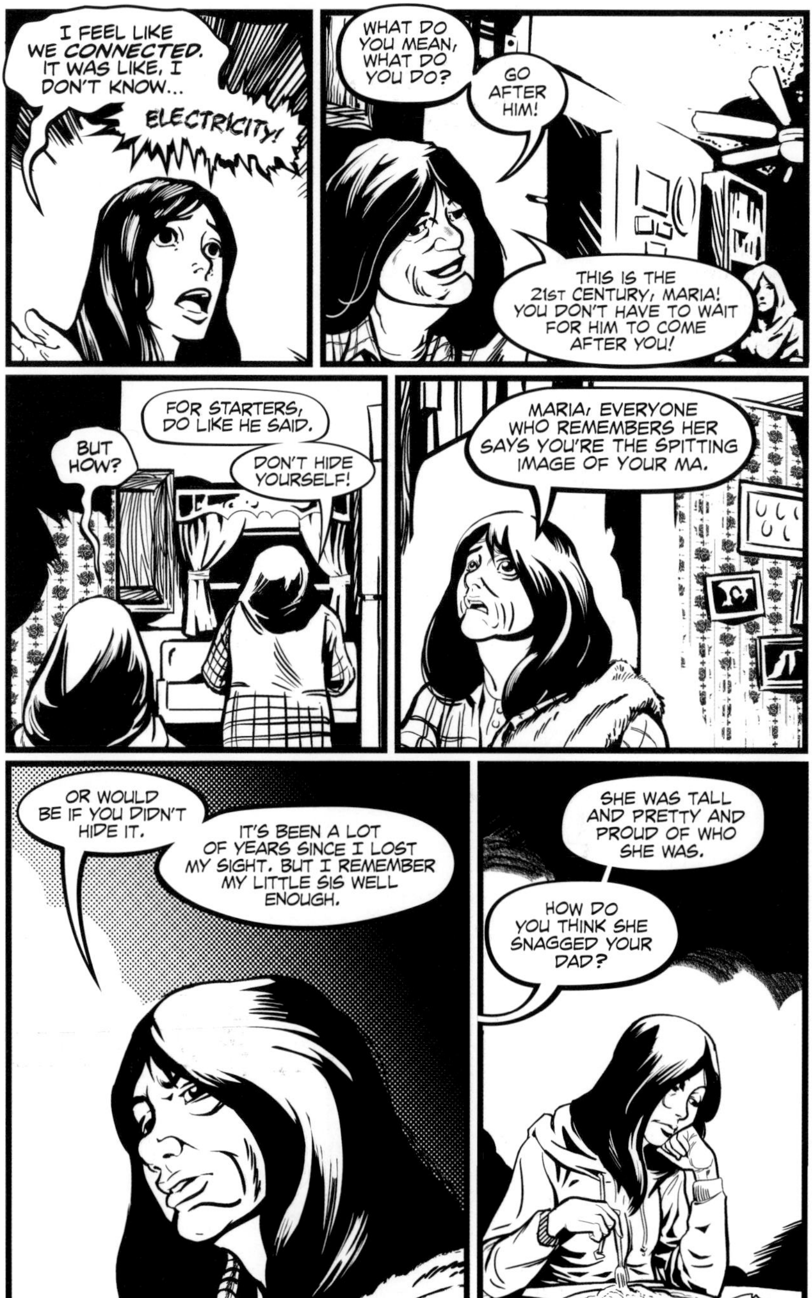
I FEEL LIKE WE CONNECTED. IT WAS LIKE, I DON'T KNOW...
ELECTRICITY!
WHAT DO YOU MEAN, WHAT DO YOU DO?
GO AFTER HIM!
THIS IS THE 21st CENTURY, MARIA! YOU DON'T HAVE TO WAIT FOR HIM TO COME AFTER YOU!
BUT HOW?
FOR STARTERS, DO LIKE HE SAID.
DON'T HIDE YOURSELF!
MARIA, EVERYONE WHO REMEMBERS HER SAYS YOU'RE THE SPITTING IMAGE OF YOUR MA.
OR WOULD BE IF YOU DIDN'T HIDE IT.
IT'S BEEN A LOT OF YEARS SINCE I LOST MY SIGHT. BUT I REMEMBER MY LITTLE SIS WELL ENOUGH.
SHE WAS TALL AND PRETTY AND PROUD OF WHO SHE WAS.
HOW DO YOU THINK SHE SNAGGED YOUR DAD?

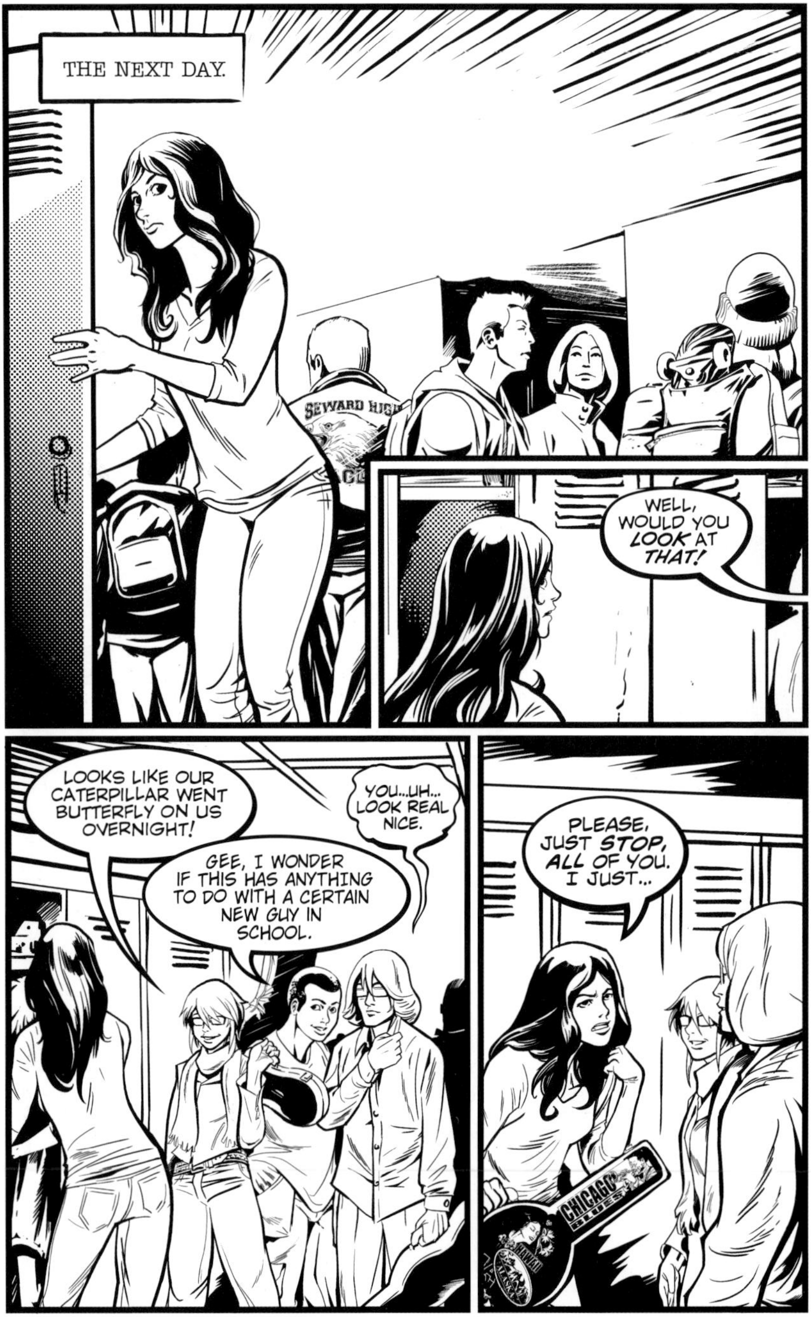
THE NEXT DAY.
SEWARD HIGH
WELL, WOULD YOU LOOK AT THAT!
LOOKS LIKE OUR CATERPILLAR WENT BUTTERFLY ON US OVERNIGHT!
YOU...UH... LOOK REAL NICE.
GEE, I WONDER IF THIS HAS ANYTHING TO DO WITH A CERTAIN NEW GUY IN SCHOOL.
PLEASE, JUST STOP, ALL OF YOU. I JUST...
CHICAGO BLUES

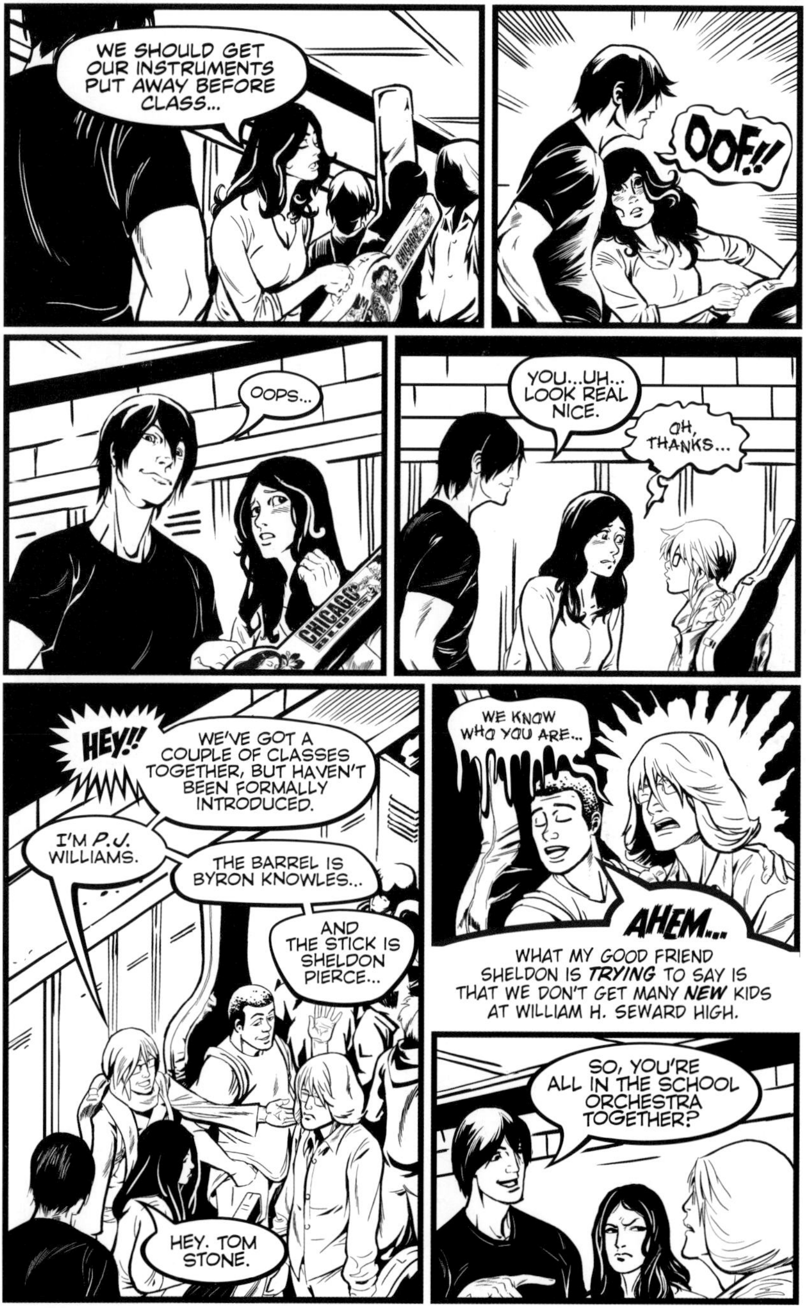
WE SHOULD GET OUR INSTRUMENTS PUT AWAY BEFORE CLASS...
CHICAGO
OOF!!
OOPS...
CHICAGO BLUES
YOU...UH... LOOK REAL NICE.
OH, THANKS...
HEY!!
WE'VE GOT A COUPLE OF CLASSES TOGETHER, BUT HAVEN'T BEEN FORMALLY INTRODUCED.
I'M P.J. WILLIAMS.
THE BARREL IS BYRON KNOWLES...
AND THE STICK IS SHELDON PIERCE...
HEY. TOM STONE.
WE KNOW WHO YOU ARE...
AHEM...
WHAT MY GOOD FRIEND SHELDON IS TRYING TO SAY IS THAT WE DON'T GET MANY NEW KIDS AT WILLIAM H. SEWARD HIGH.
SO, YOU'RE ALL IN THE SCHOOL ORCHESTRA TOGETHER?

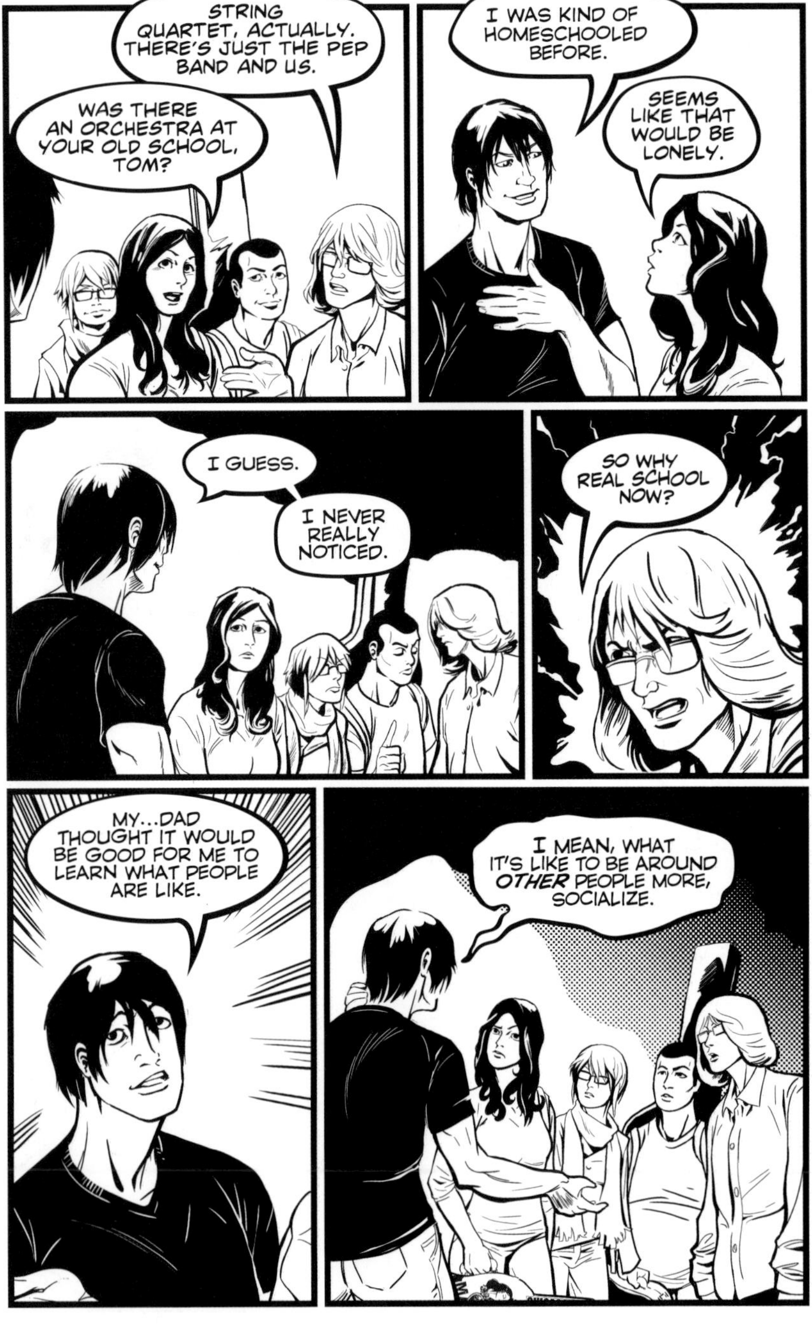
WAS THERE AN ORCHESTRA AT YOUR OLD SCHOOL, TOM?
STRING QUARTET, ACTUALLY. THERE'S JUST THE PEP BAND AND US.
I WAS KIND OF HOMESCHOOLED BEFORE.
SEEMS LIKE THAT WOULD BE LONELY.
I GUESS.
I NEVER REALLY NOTICED.
SO WHY REAL SCHOOL NOW?
MY...DAD THOUGHT IT WOULD BE GOOD FOR ME TO LEARN WHAT PEOPLE ARE LIKE.
I MEAN, WHAT IT'S LIKE TO BE AROUND *OTHER* PEOPLE MORE, SOCIALIZE.

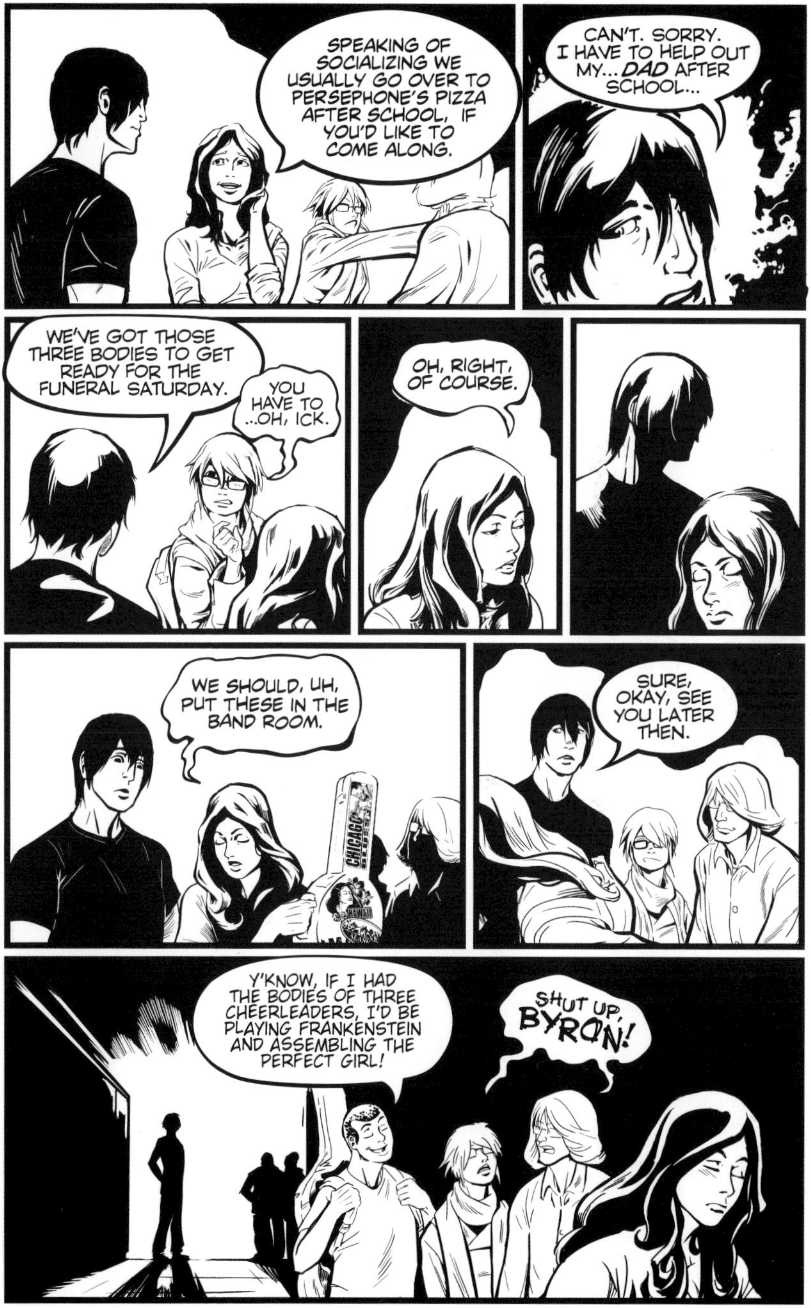
SPEAKING OF SOCIALIZING WE USUALLY GO OVER TO PERSEPHONE'S PIZZA AFTER SCHOOL, IF YOU'D LIKE TO COME ALONG.
CAN'T. SORRY. I HAVE TO HELP OUT MY... DAD AFTER SCHOOL...
WE'VE GOT THOSE THREE BODIES TO GET READY FOR THE FUNERAL SATURDAY.
YOU HAVE TO ...OH, ICK.
OH, RIGHT, OF COURSE.
WE SHOULD, UH, PUT THESE IN THE BAND ROOM.
CHICAGO
HAWAII
SURE, OKAY, SEE YOU LATER THEN.
Y'KNOW, IF I HAD THE BODIES OF THREE CHEERLEADERS, I'D BE PLAYING FRANKENSTEIN AND ASSEMBLING THE PERFECT GIRL!
SHUT UP, BYRON!

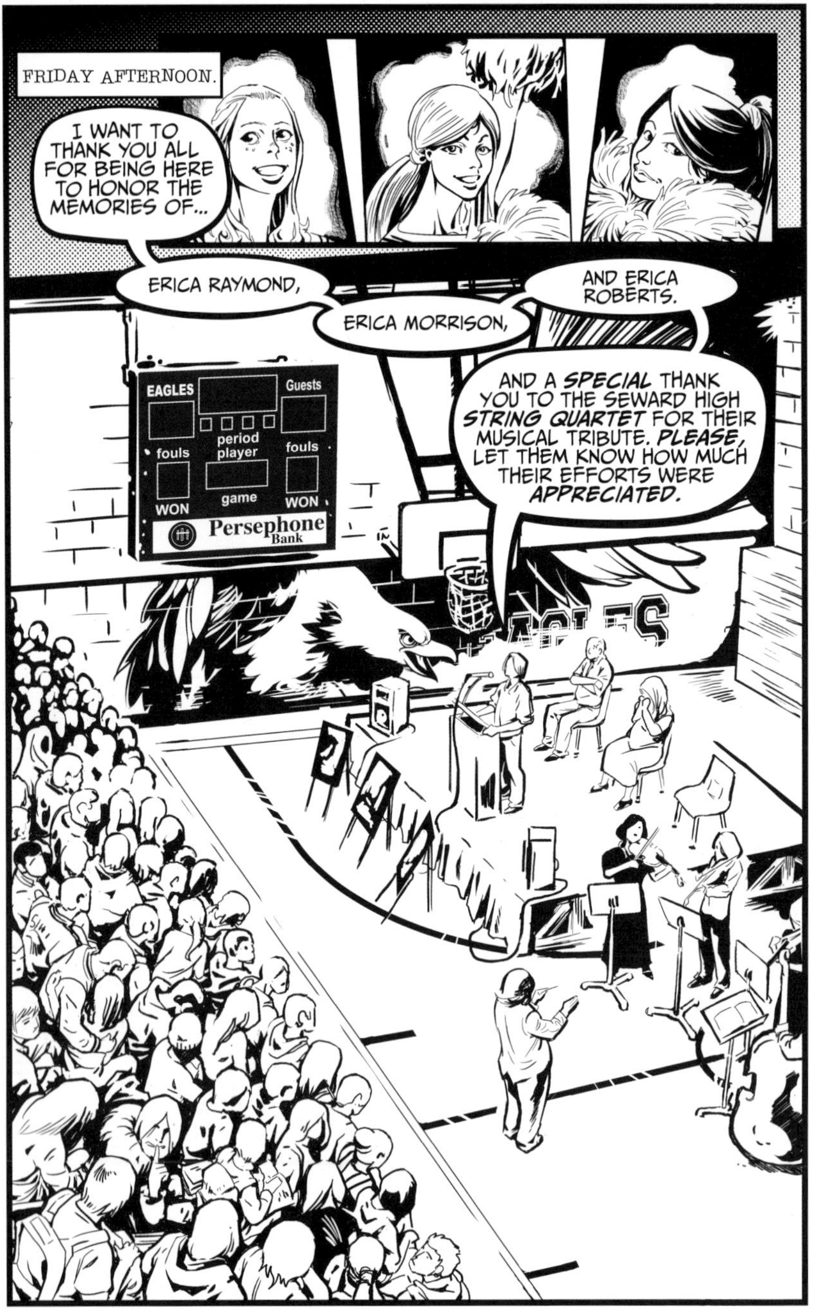
FRIDAY AFTERNOON.
I WANT TO THANK YOU ALL FOR BEING HERE TO HONOR THE MEMORIES OF...
ERICA RAYMOND,
ERICA MORRISON,
AND ERICA ROBERTS.
AND A SPECIAL THANK YOU TO THE SEWARD HIGH STRING QUARTET FOR THEIR MUSICAL TRIBUTE. PLEASE, LET THEM KNOW HOW MUCH THEIR EFFORTS WERE APPRECIATED.
EAGLES
Guests
period
player
fouls
fouls
game
WON
WON
Persephone Bank
EAGLES

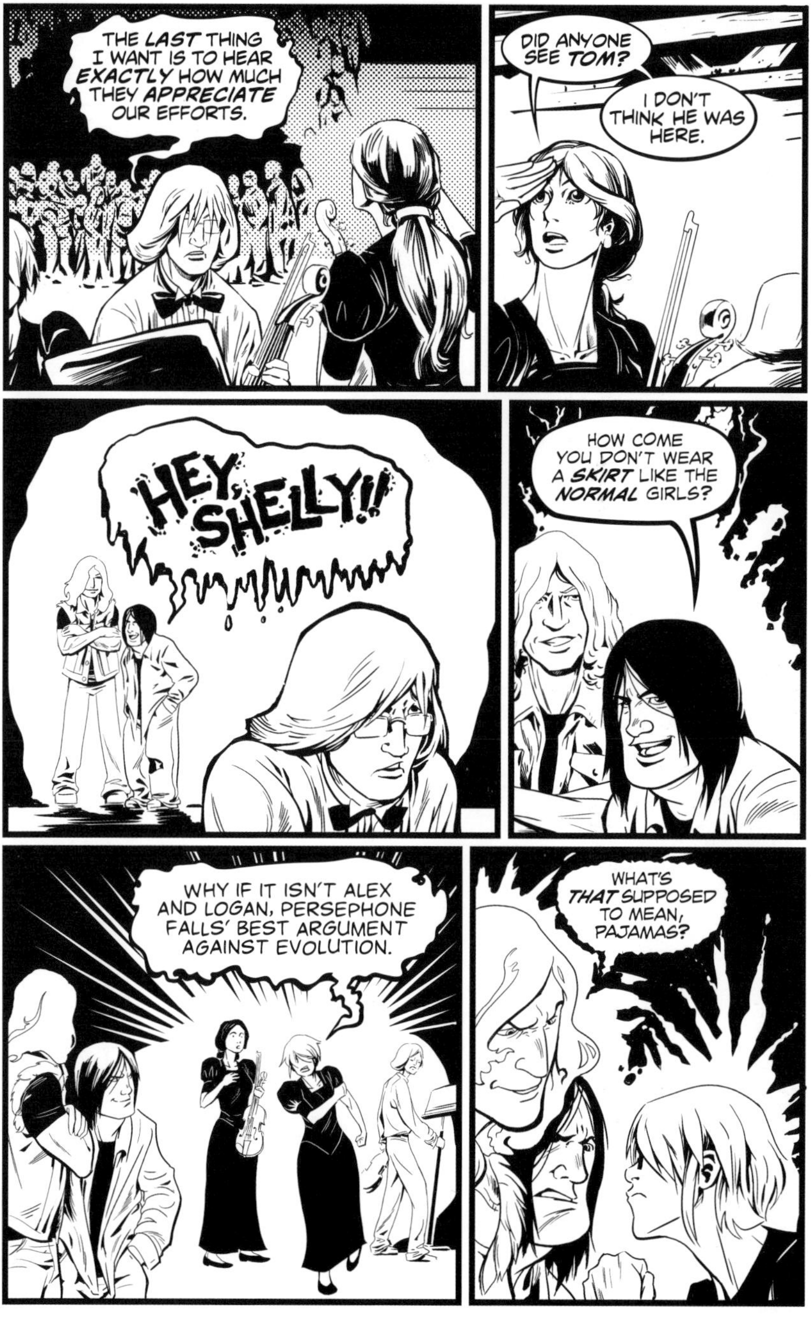
THE LAST THING I WANT IS TO HEAR EXACTLY HOW MUCH THEY APPRECIATE OUR EFFORTS.
DID ANYONE SEE TOM?
I DON'T THINK HE WAS HERE.
HEY, SHELLY!!
HOW COME YOU DON'T WEAR A SKIRT LIKE THE NORMAL GIRLS?
WHY IF IT ISN'T ALEX AND LOGAN, PERSEPHONE FALLS' BEST ARGUMENT AGAINST EVOLUTION.
WHAT'S THAT SUPPOSED TO MEAN, PAJAMAS?

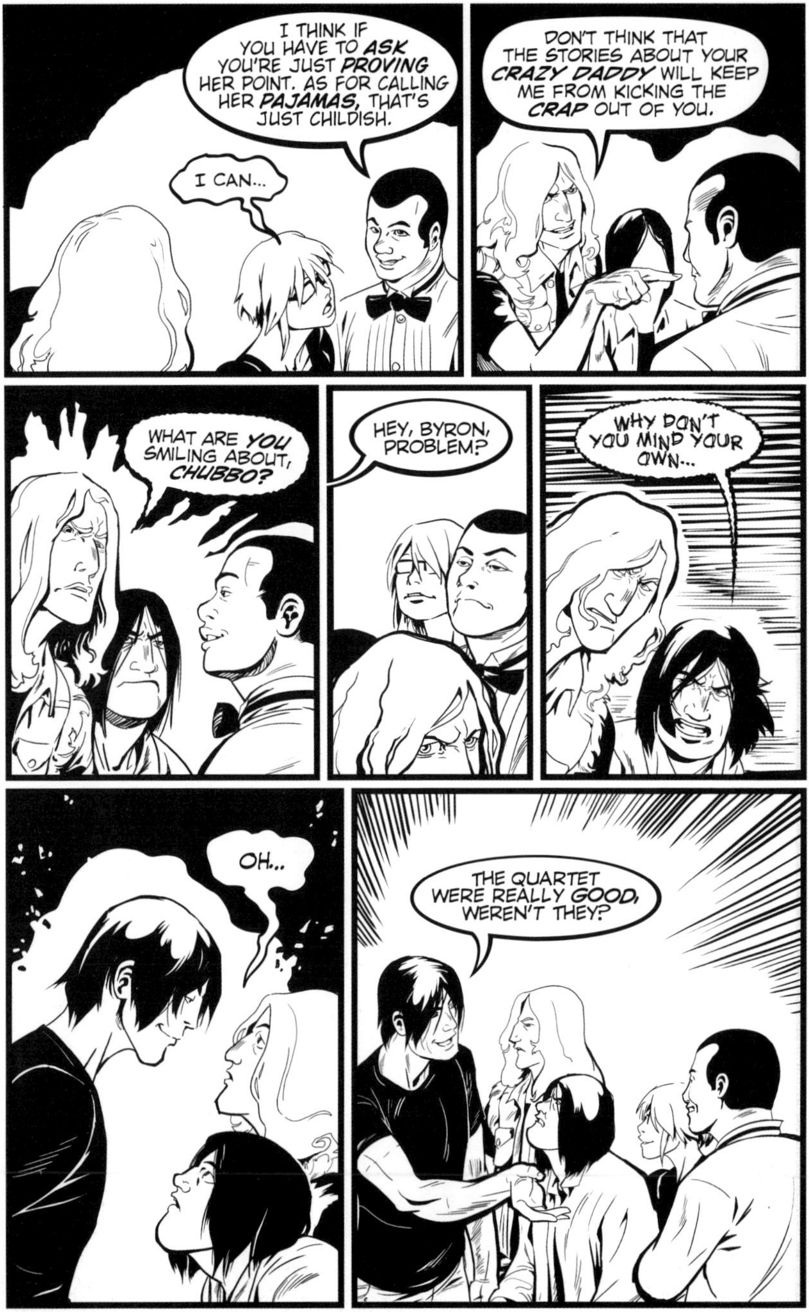
I THINK IF YOU HAVE TO ASK YOU'RE JUST PROVING HER POINT. AS FOR CALLING HER PAJAMAS, THAT'S JUST CHILDISH.
I CAN...
DON'T THINK THAT THE STORIES ABOUT YOUR CRAZY DADDY WILL KEEP ME FROM KICKING THE CRAP OUT OF YOU.
WHAT ARE YOU SMILING ABOUT, CHUBBO?
HEY, BYRON, PROBLEM?
WHY DON'T YOU MIND YOUR OWN...
OH...
THE QUARTET WERE REALLY GOOD, WEREN'T THEY?

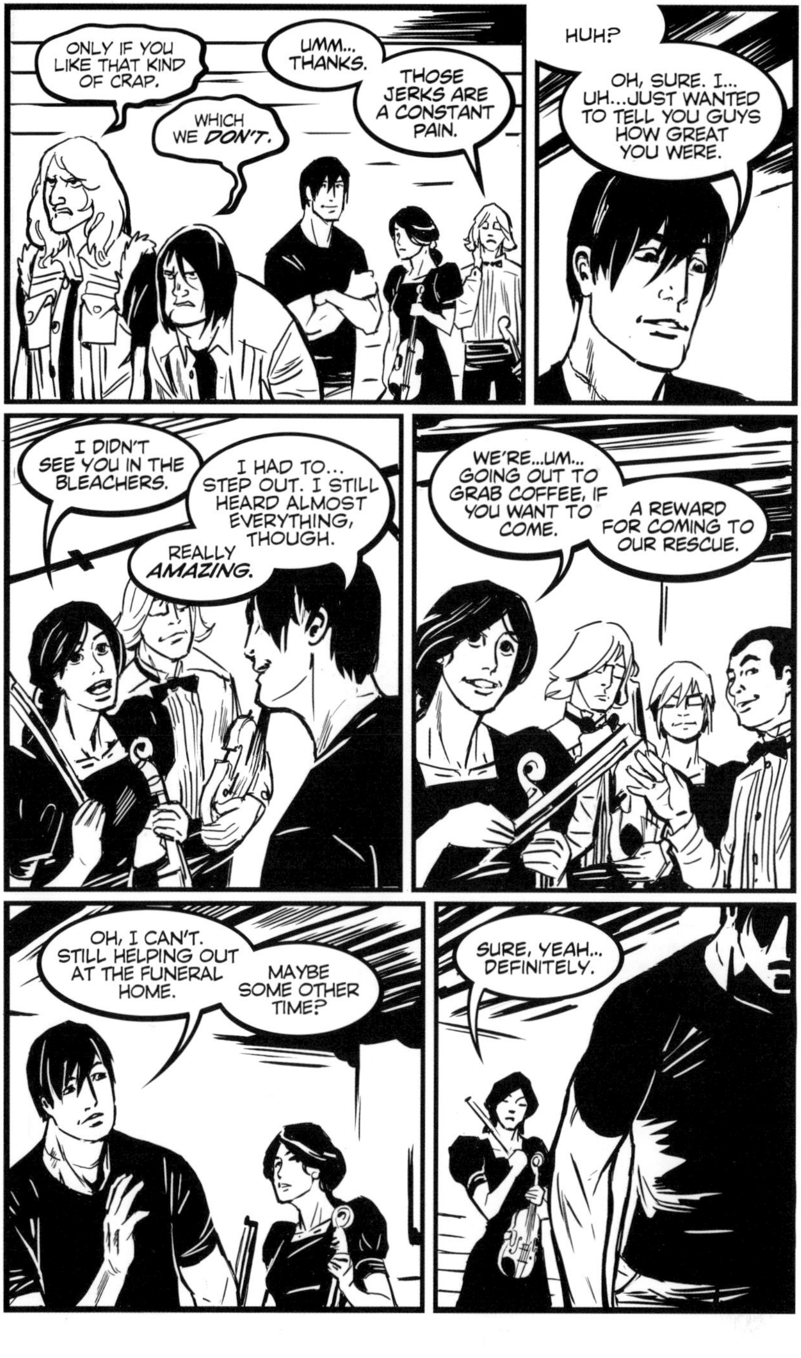
ONLY IF YOU LIKE THAT KIND OF CRAP.
WHICH WE DON'T.
UMM... THANKS.
THOSE JERKS ARE A CONSTANT PAIN.
HUH?
OH, SURE. I... UH...JUST WANTED TO TELL YOU GUYS HOW GREAT YOU WERE.
I DIDN'T SEE YOU IN THE BLEACHERS.
I HAD TO... STEP OUT. I STILL HEARD ALMOST EVERYTHING, THOUGH.
REALLY AMAZING.
WE'RE...UM... GOING OUT TO GRAB COFFEE, IF YOU WANT TO COME.
A REWARD FOR COMING TO OUR RESCUE.
OH, I CAN'T. STILL HELPING OUT AT THE FUNERAL HOME.
MAYBE SOME OTHER TIME?
SURE, YEAH... DEFINITELY.

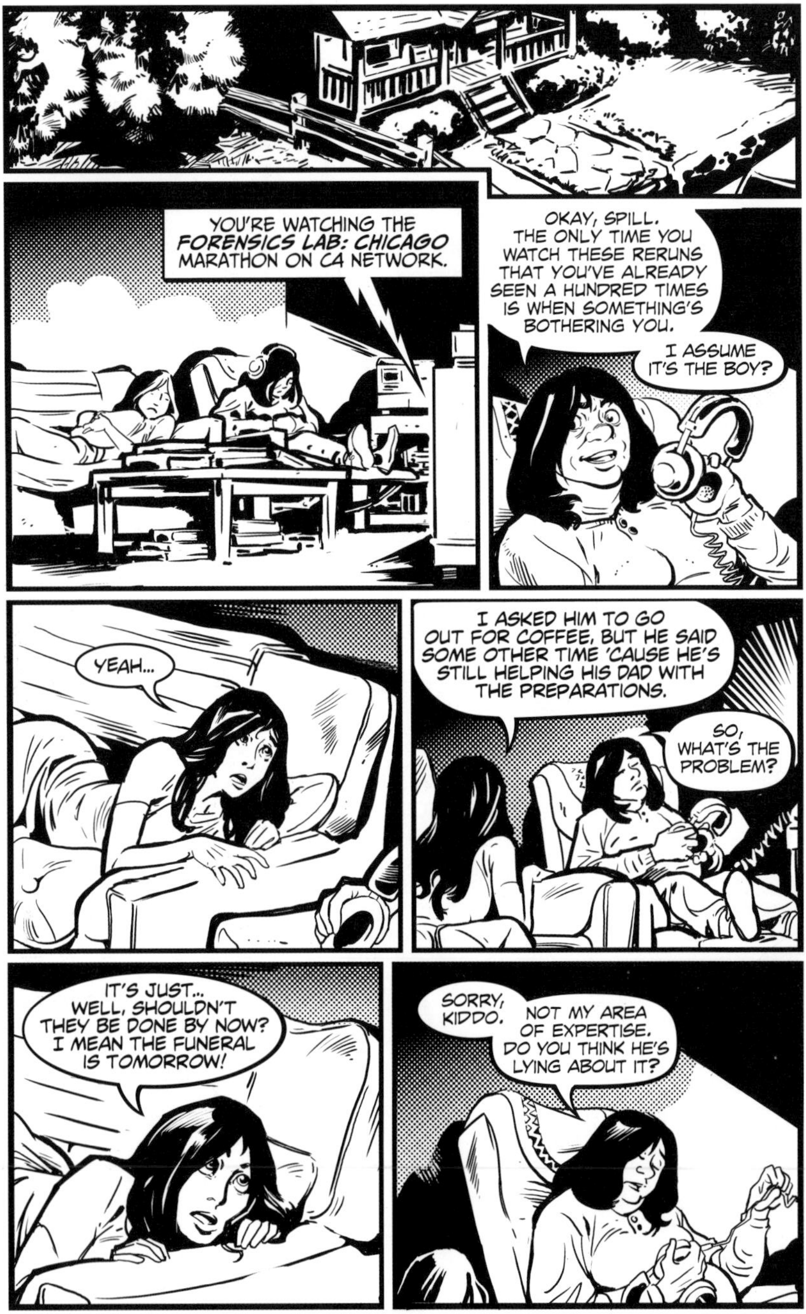
YOU'RE WATCHING THE *FORENSICS LAB: CHICAGO* MARATHON ON C4 NETWORK.
OKAY, SPILL. THE ONLY TIME YOU WATCH THESE RERUNS THAT YOU'VE ALREADY SEEN A HUNDRED TIMES IS WHEN SOMETHING'S BOTHERING YOU.
I ASSUME IT'S THE BOY?
YEAH...
I ASKED HIM TO GO OUT FOR COFFEE, BUT HE SAID SOME OTHER TIME 'CAUSE HE'S STILL HELPING HIS DAD WITH THE PREPARATIONS.
SO, WHAT'S THE PROBLEM?
IT'S JUST... WELL, SHOULDN'T THEY BE DONE BY NOW? I MEAN THE FUNERAL IS TOMORROW!
SORRY, KIDDO.
NOT MY AREA OF EXPERTISE. DO YOU THINK HE'S LYING ABOUT IT?

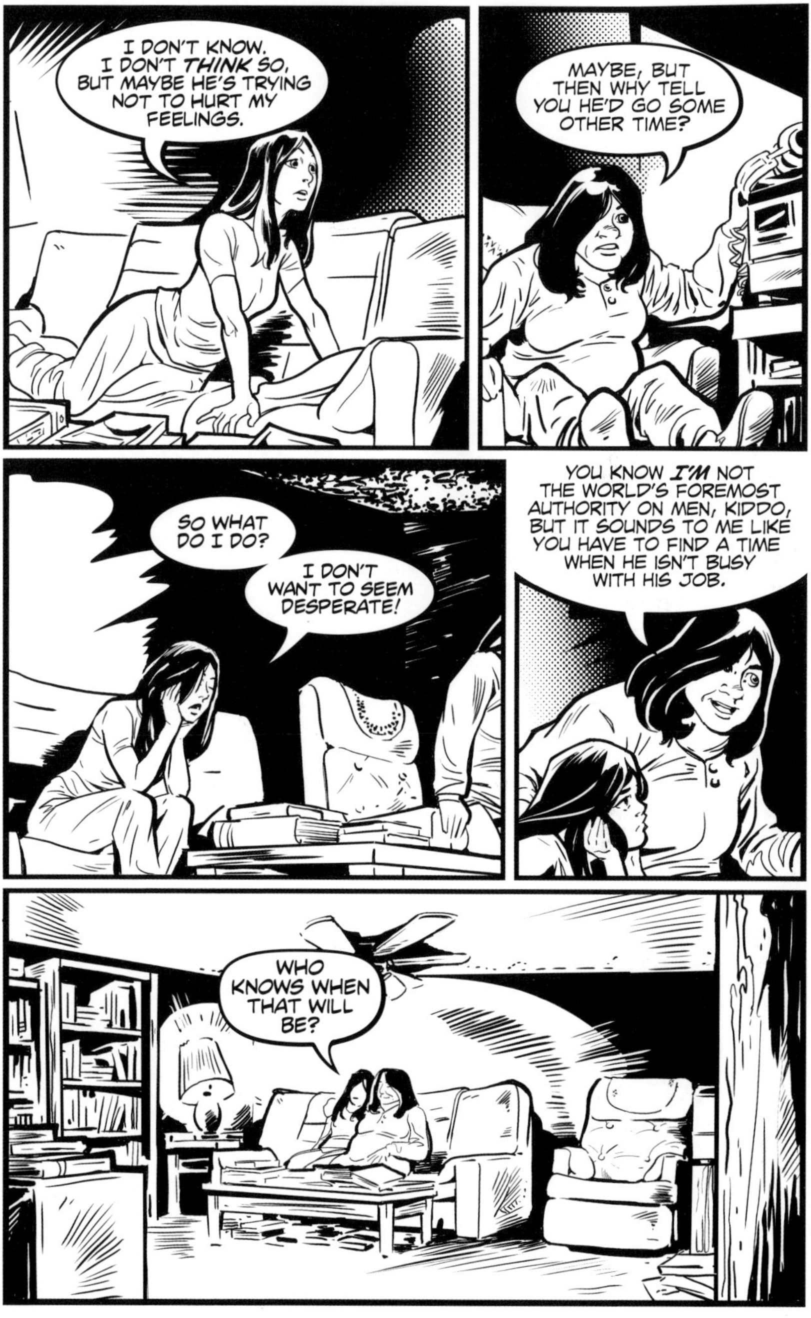
I DON'T KNOW. I DON'T THINK SO, BUT MAYBE HE'S TRYING NOT TO HURT MY FEELINGS.
MAYBE, BUT THEN WHY TELL YOU HE'D GO SOME OTHER TIME?
SO WHAT DO I DO?
I DON'T WANT TO SEEM DESPERATE!
YOU KNOW I'M NOT THE WORLD'S FOREMOST AUTHORITY ON MEN, KIDDO, BUT IT SOUNDS TO ME LIKE YOU HAVE TO FIND A TIME WHEN HE ISN'T BUSY WITH HIS JOB.
WHO KNOWS WHEN THAT WILL BE?

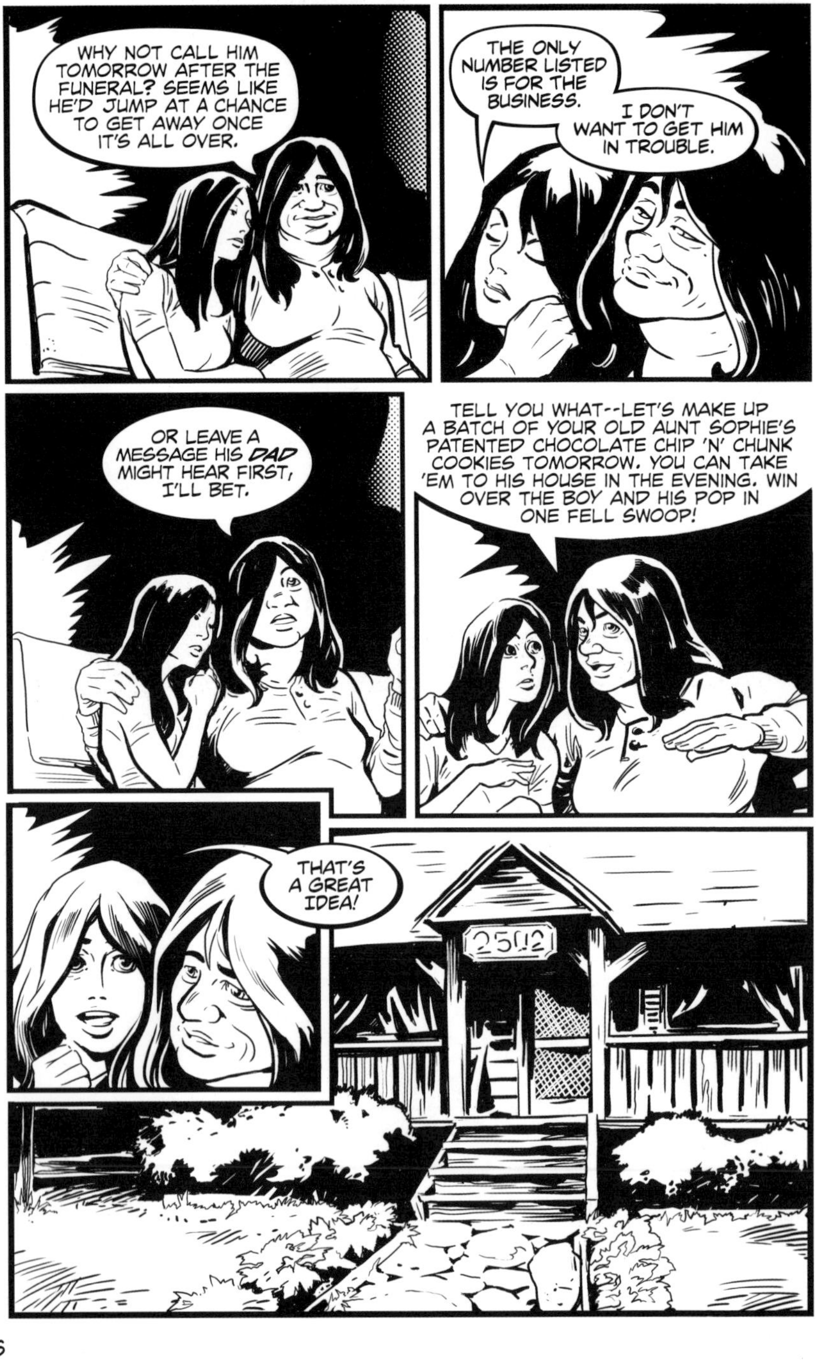
WHY NOT CALL HIM TOMORROW AFTER THE FUNERAL? SEEMS LIKE HE'D JUMP AT A CHANCE TO GET AWAY ONCE IT'S ALL OVER.
THE ONLY NUMBER LISTED IS FOR THE BUSINESS.
I DON'T WANT TO GET HIM IN TROUBLE.
OR LEAVE A MESSAGE HIS *DAD* MIGHT HEAR FIRST, I'LL BET.
TELL YOU WHAT--LET'S MAKE UP A BATCH OF YOUR OLD AUNT SOPHIE'S PATENTED CHOCOLATE CHIP 'N' CHUNK COOKIES TOMORROW. YOU CAN TAKE 'EM TO HIS HOUSE IN THE EVENING. WIN OVER THE BOY AND HIS POP IN ONE FELL SWOOP!
THAT'S A GREAT IDEA!
2502

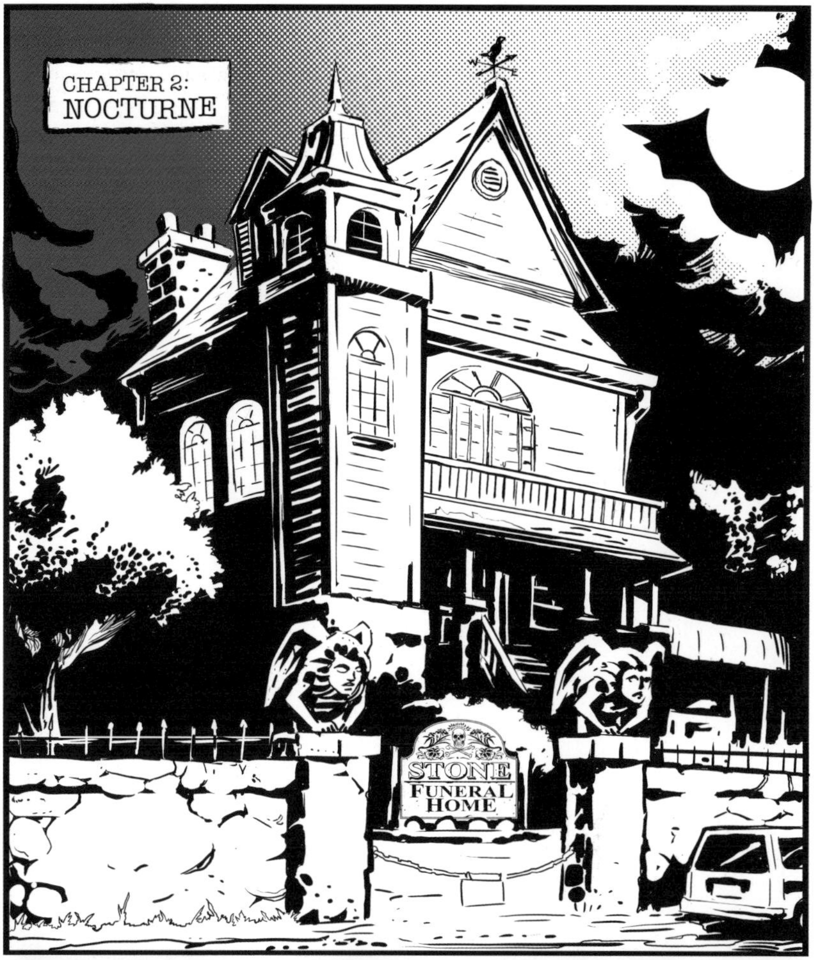
CHAPTER 2:
NOCTURNE
STONE
FUNERAL
HOME

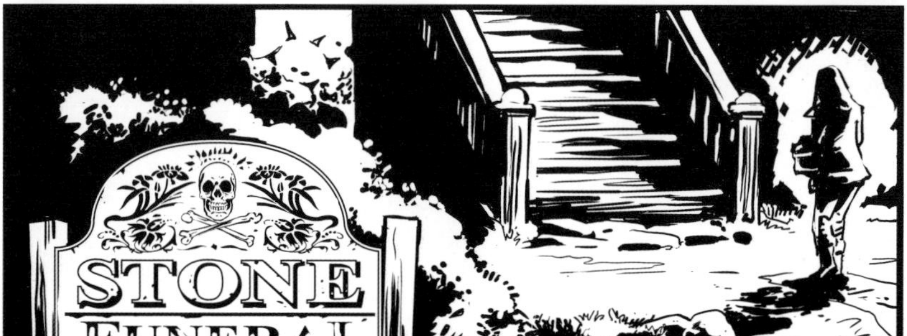
STONE
FUNERAL

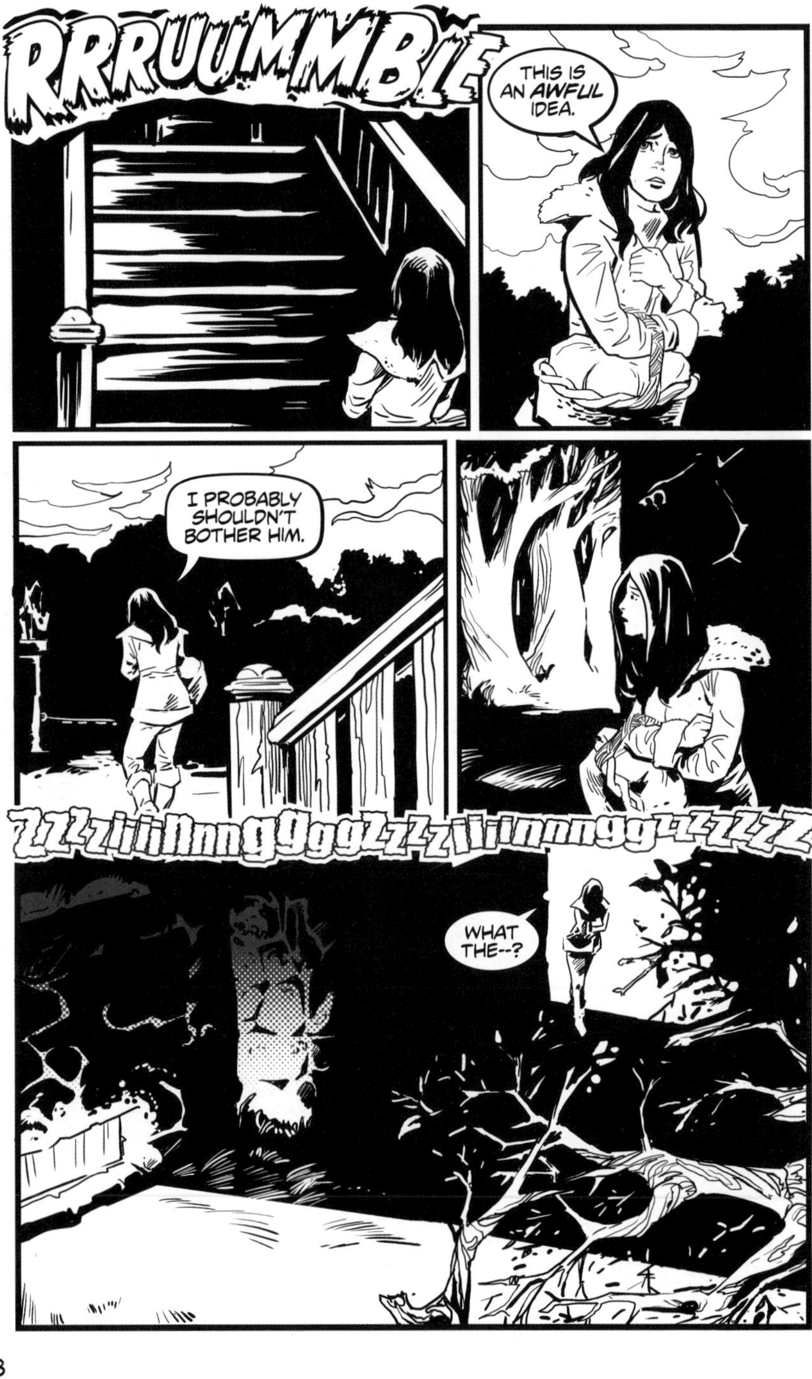
RRRUUMMBLE
THIS IS AN AWFUL IDEA.
I PROBABLY SHOULDN'T BOTHER HIM.
ZZZZIIIINNNGGGGZZZZIIIINNNGGZZZZZZ
WHAT THE--?

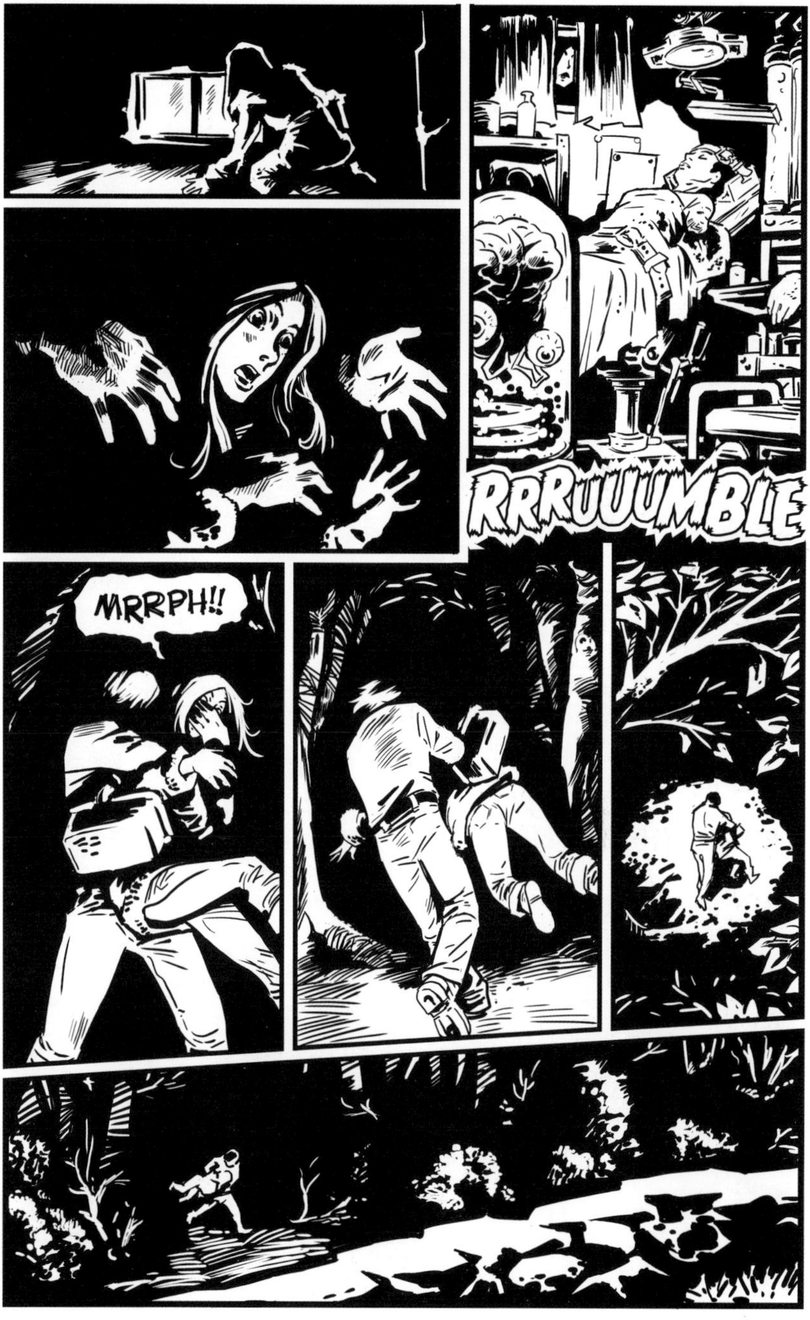
RRRUUUMBLE
MRRPH!!

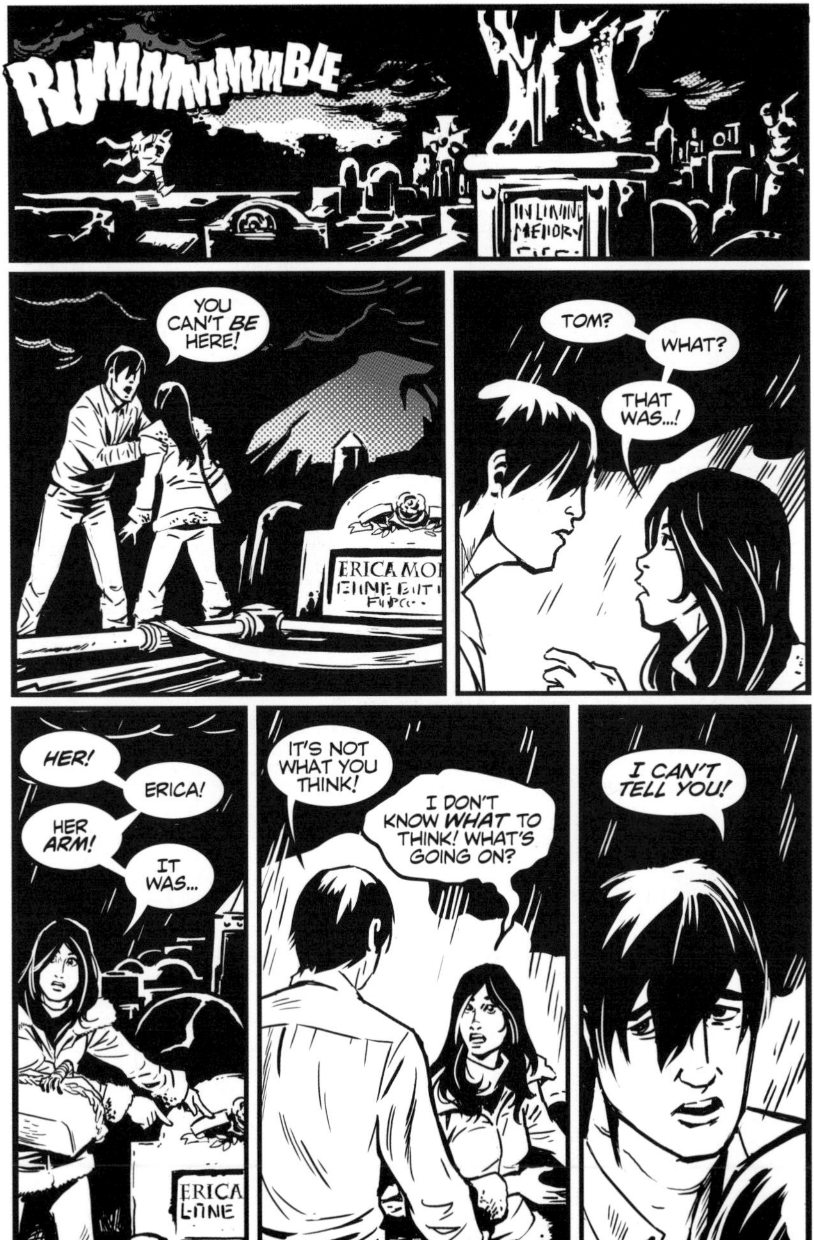

RUMMMMMMBLE
IN LOVING MEMORY
YOU CAN'T *BE* HERE!
TOM?
WHAT?
THAT WAS...!
HER!
ERICA!
HER *ARM!*
IT WAS...
IT'S NOT WHAT YOU THINK!
I DON'T KNOW ***WHAT*** TO THINK! WHAT'S GOING ON?
I CAN'T TELL YOU!

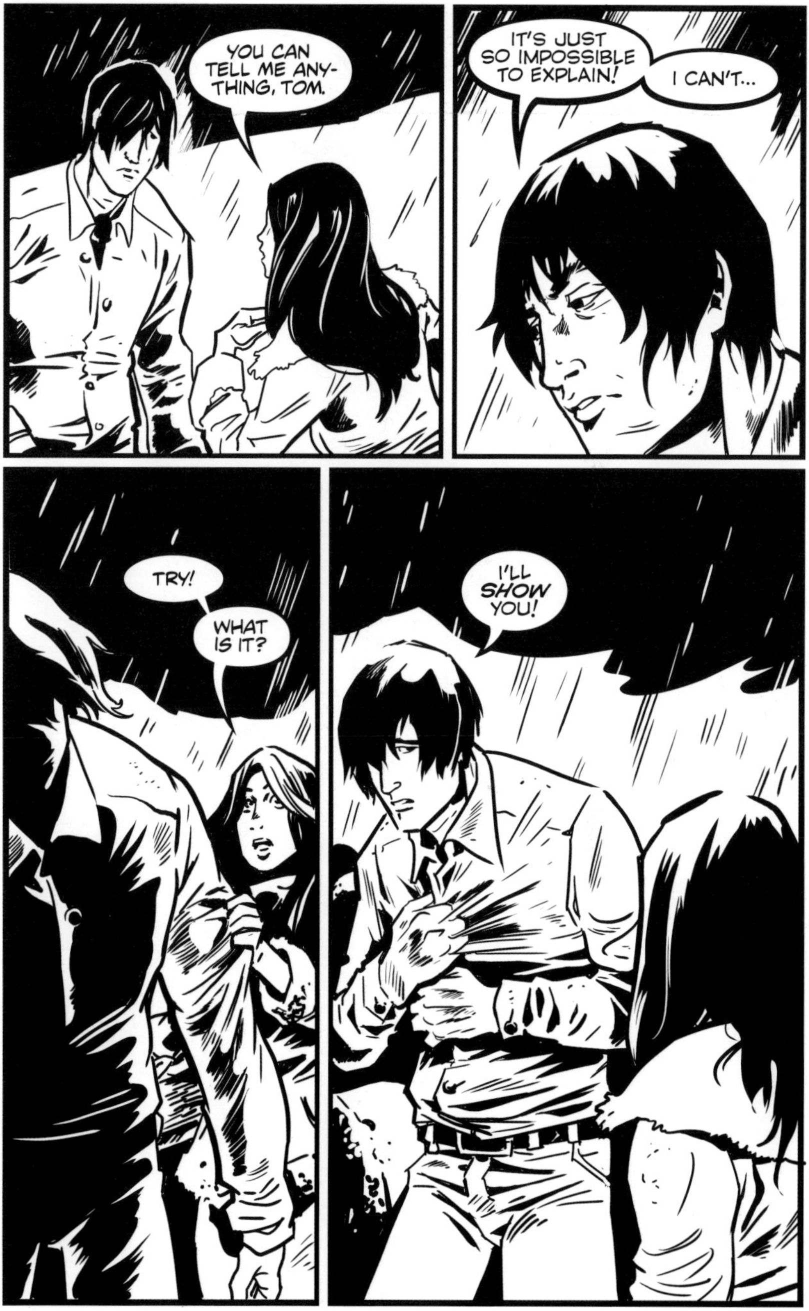
YOU CAN TELL ME ANYTHING, TOM.
IT'S JUST SO IMPOSSIBLE TO EXPLAIN!
I CAN'T...
TRY!
WHAT IS IT?
I'LL SHOW YOU!

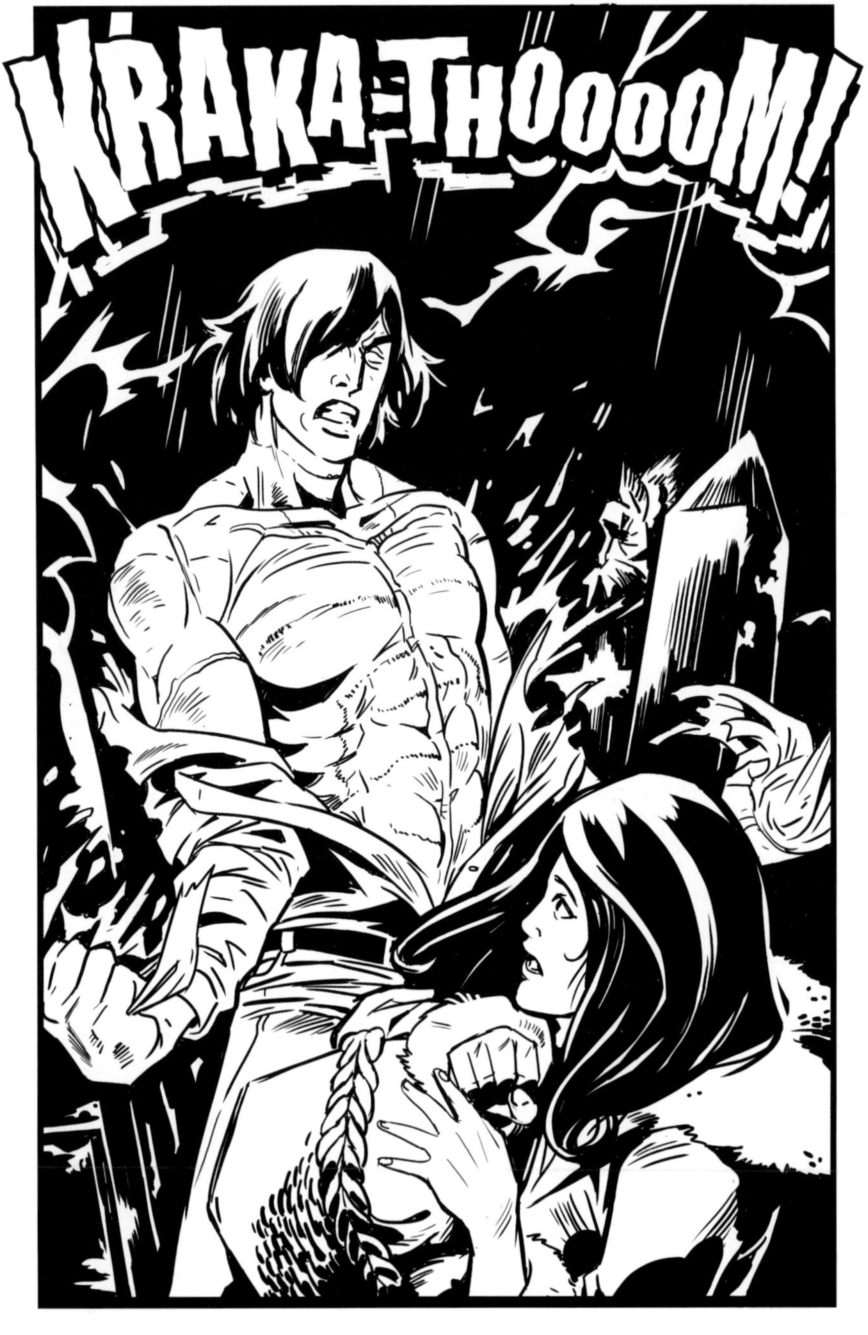
KRAKA-THOOOOOM!!

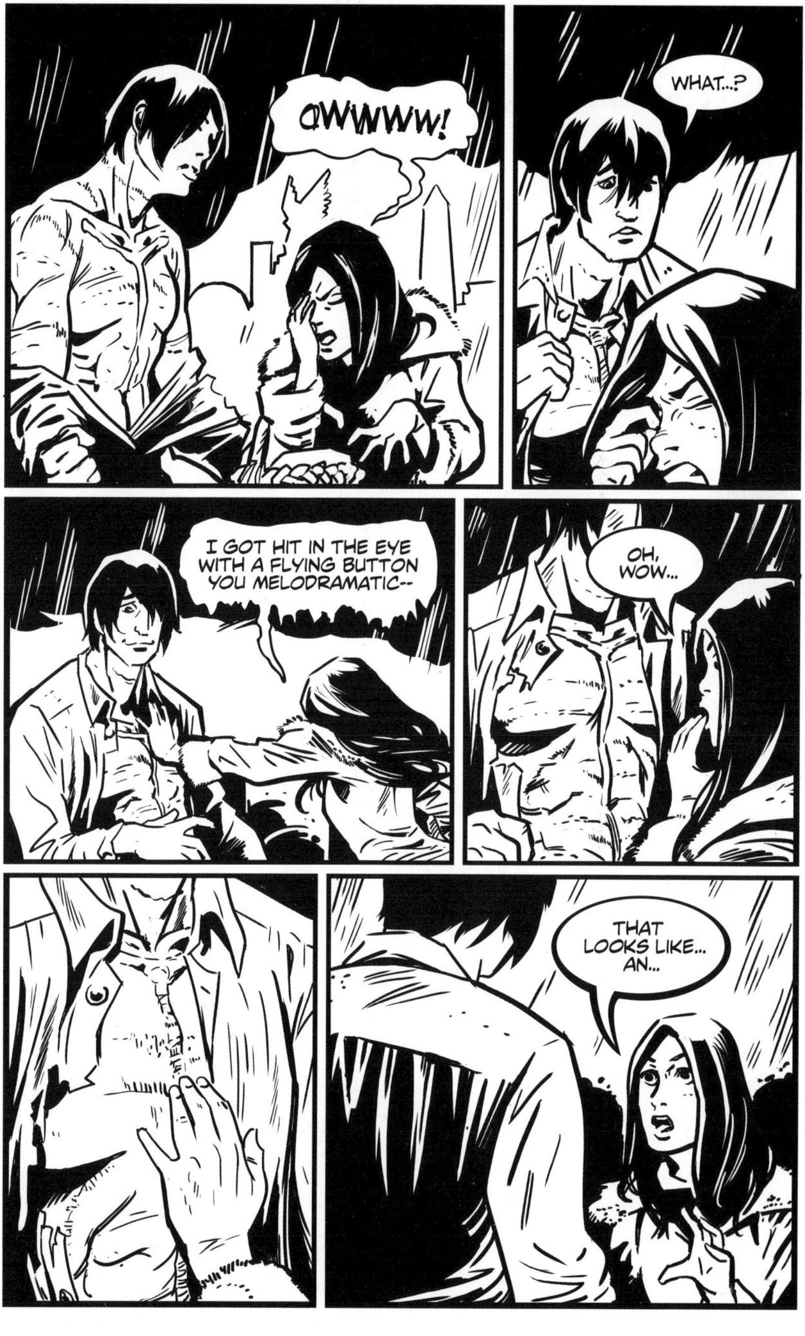
OWWWW!
WHAT...?
I GOT HIT IN THE EYE WITH A FLYING BUTTON YOU MELODRAMATIC--
OH, WOW...
THAT LOOKS LIKE... AN...

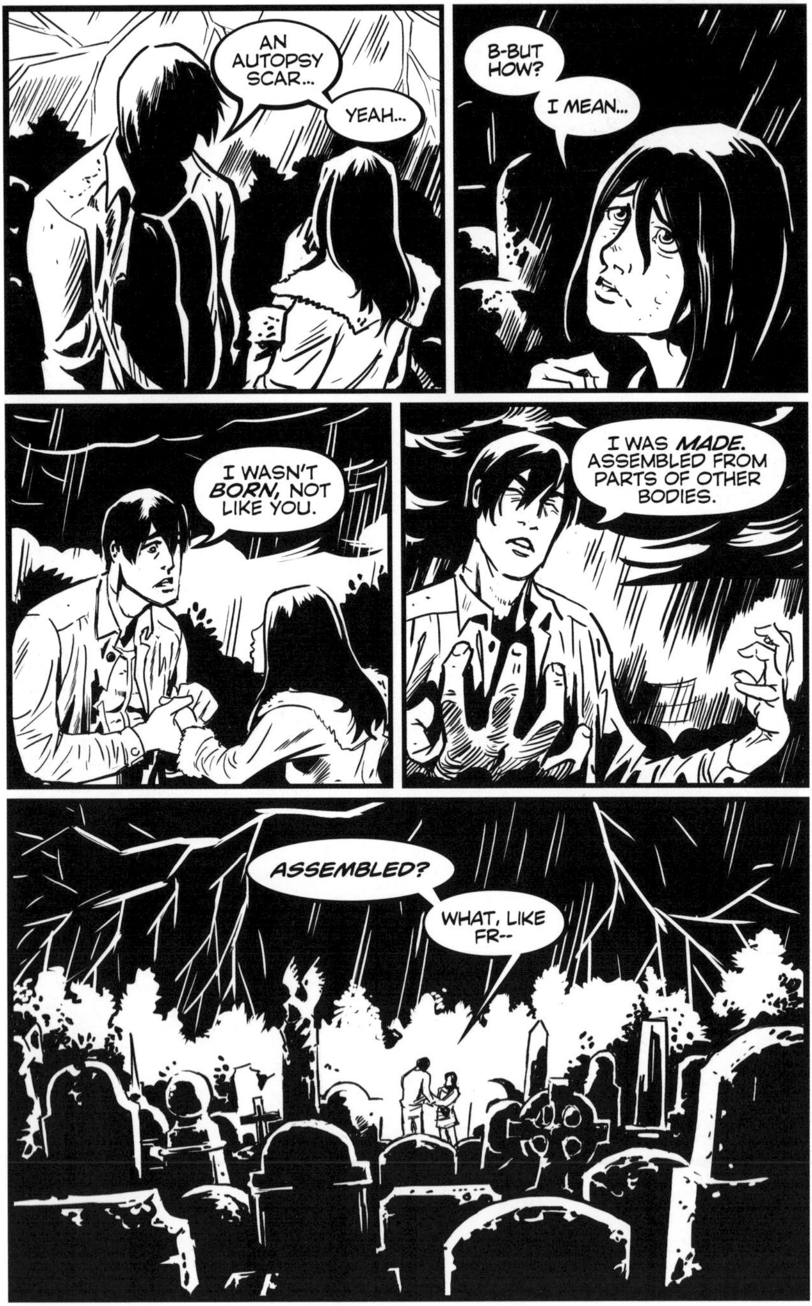
AN AUTOPSY SCAR...
YEAH...
B-BUT HOW?
I MEAN...
I WASN'T BORN, NOT LIKE YOU.
I WAS MADE. ASSEMBLED FROM PARTS OF OTHER BODIES.
ASSEMBLED?
WHAT, LIKE FR--

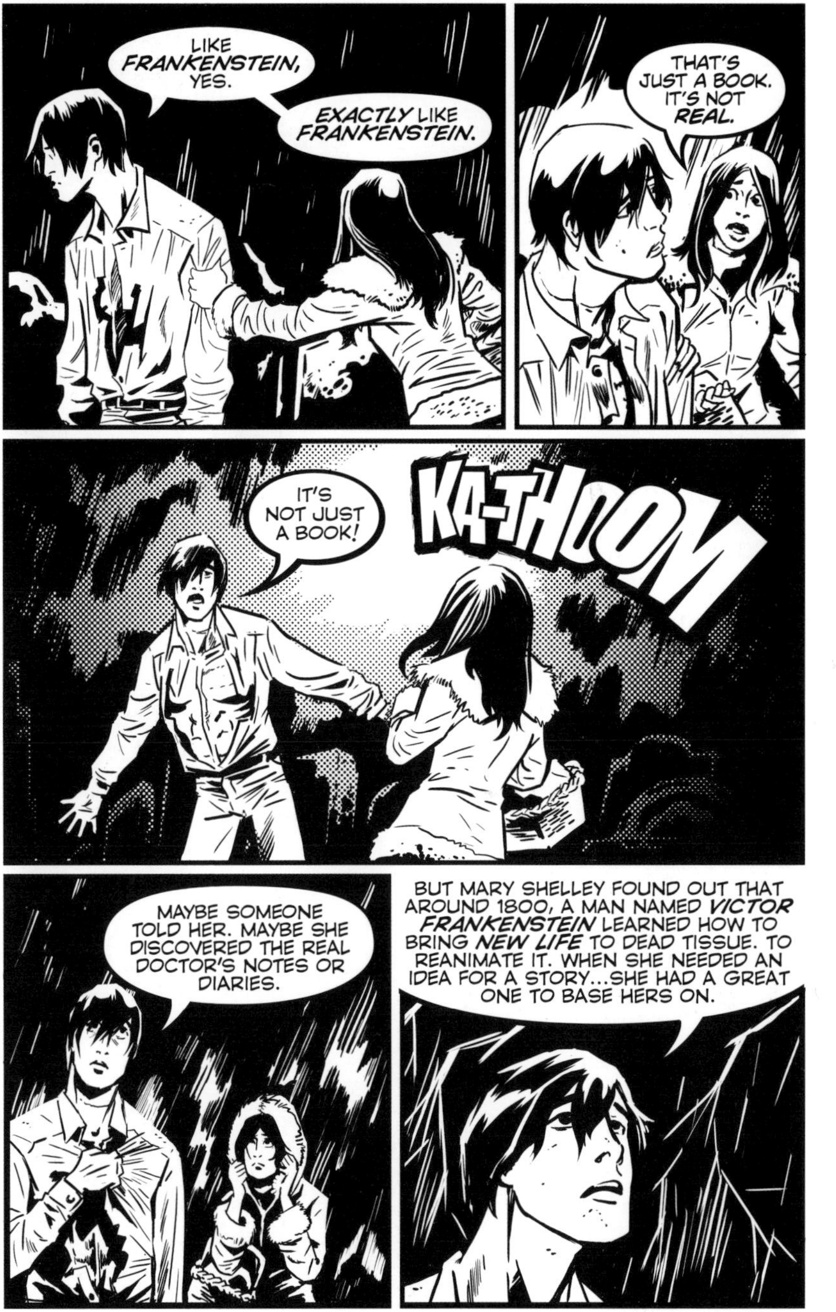
LIKE FRANKENSTEIN, YES.
EXACTLY LIKE FRANKENSTEIN.
THAT'S JUST A BOOK. IT'S NOT REAL.
IT'S NOT JUST A BOOK!
KA-THOOM
MAYBE SOMEONE TOLD HER. MAYBE SHE DISCOVERED THE REAL DOCTOR'S NOTES OR DIARIES.
BUT MARY SHELLEY FOUND OUT THAT AROUND 1800, A MAN NAMED VICTOR FRANKENSTEIN LEARNED HOW TO BRING NEW LIFE TO DEAD TISSUE. TO REANIMATE IT. WHEN SHE NEEDED AN IDEA FOR A STORY...SHE HAD A GREAT ONE TO BASE HERS ON.

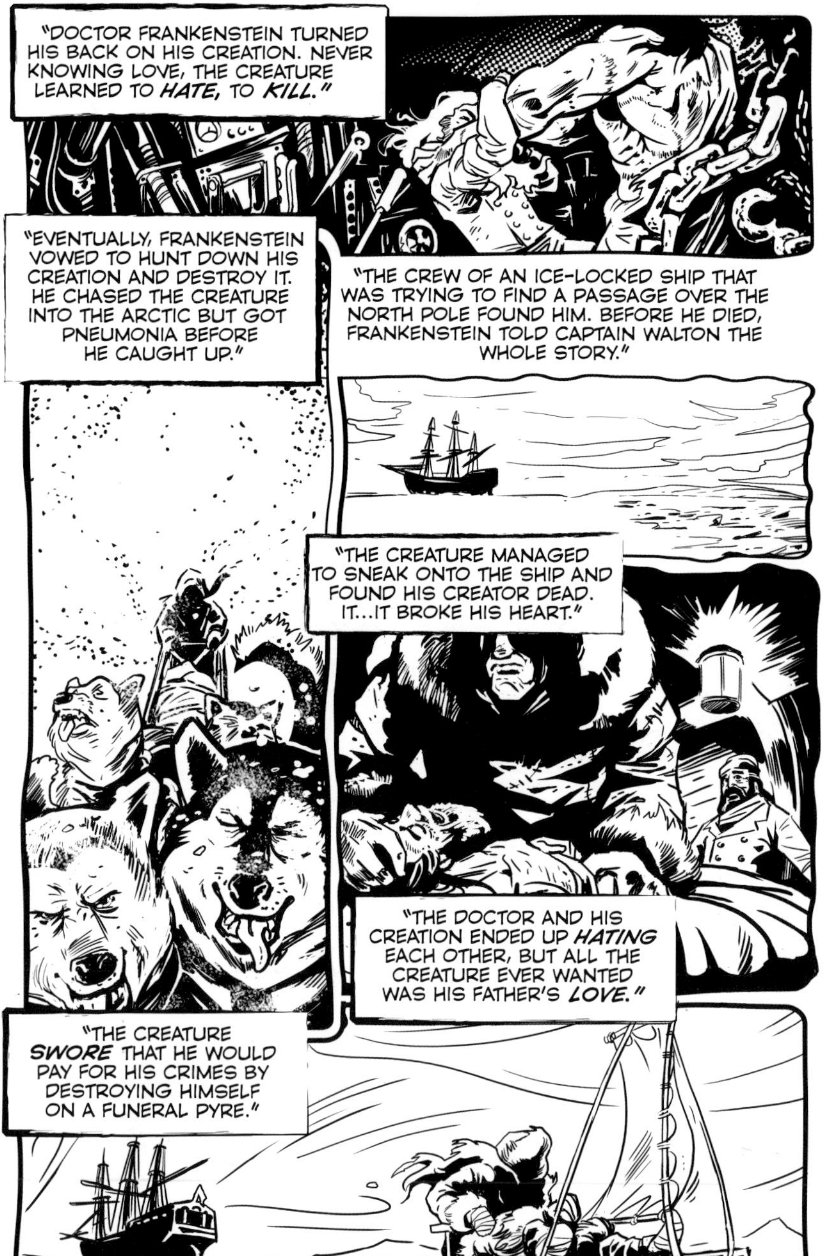
"DOCTOR FRANKENSTEIN TURNED HIS BACK ON HIS CREATION. NEVER KNOWING LOVE, THE CREATURE LEARNED TO *HATE,* TO *KILL.*"
"EVENTUALLY, FRANKENSTEIN VOWED TO HUNT DOWN HIS CREATION AND DESTROY IT. HE CHASED THE CREATURE INTO THE ARCTIC BUT GOT PNEUMONIA BEFORE HE CAUGHT UP."
"THE CREW OF AN ICE-LOCKED SHIP THAT WAS TRYING TO FIND A PASSAGE OVER THE NORTH POLE FOUND HIM. BEFORE HE DIED, FRANKENSTEIN TOLD CAPTAIN WALTON THE WHOLE STORY."
"THE CREATURE MANAGED TO SNEAK ONTO THE SHIP AND FOUND HIS CREATOR DEAD. IT...IT BROKE HIS HEART."
"THE DOCTOR AND HIS CREATION ENDED UP *HATING* EACH OTHER, BUT ALL THE CREATURE EVER WANTED WAS HIS FATHER'S *LOVE.*"
"THE CREATURE *SWORE* THAT HE WOULD PAY FOR HIS CRIMES BY DESTROYING HIMSELF ON A FUNERAL PYRE."

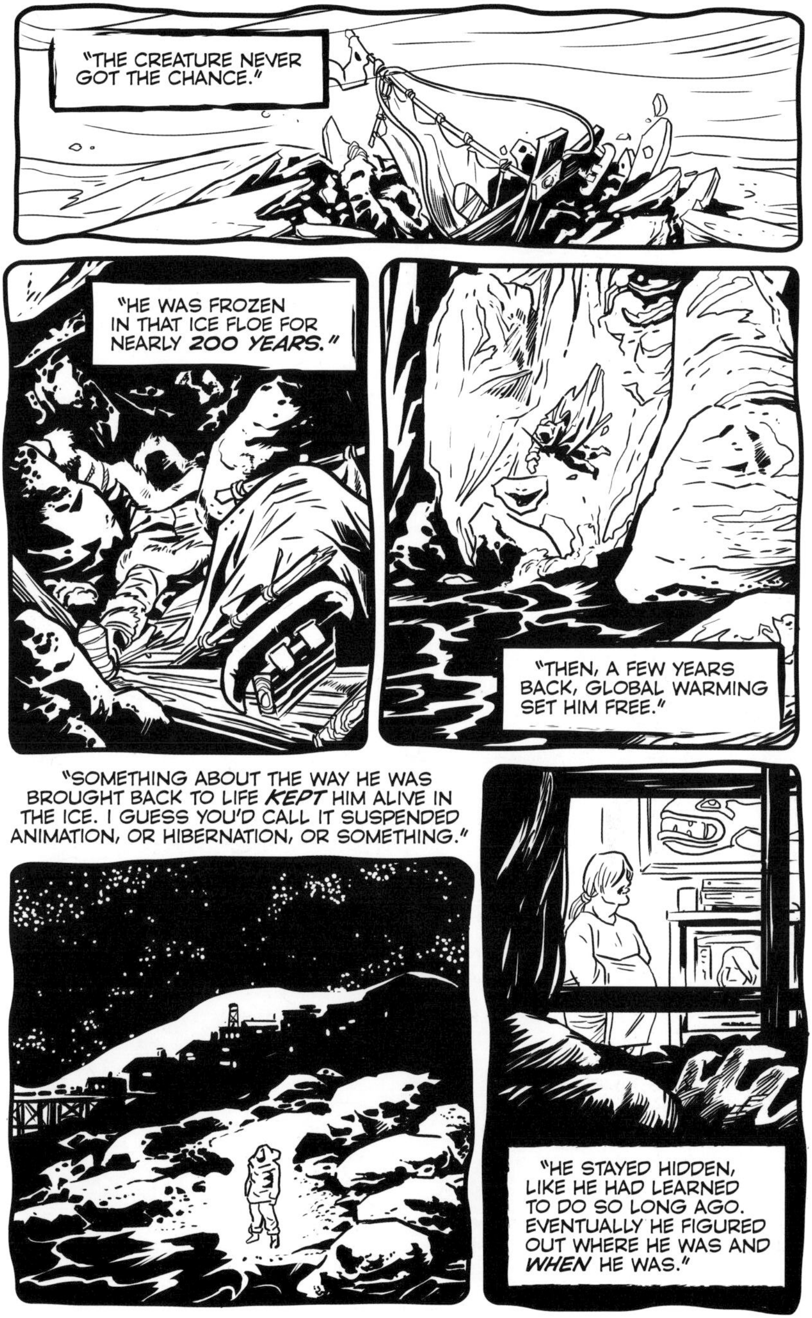
"THE CREATURE NEVER GOT THE CHANCE."
"HE WAS FROZEN IN THAT ICE FLOE FOR NEARLY 200 YEARS."
"THEN, A FEW YEARS BACK, GLOBAL WARMING SET HIM FREE."
"SOMETHING ABOUT THE WAY HE WAS BROUGHT BACK TO LIFE KEPT HIM ALIVE IN THE ICE. I GUESS YOU'D CALL IT SUSPENDED ANIMATION, OR HIBERNATION, OR SOMETHING."
"HE STAYED HIDDEN, LIKE HE HAD LEARNED TO DO SO LONG AGO. EVENTUALLY HE FIGURED OUT WHERE HE WAS AND WHEN HE WAS."

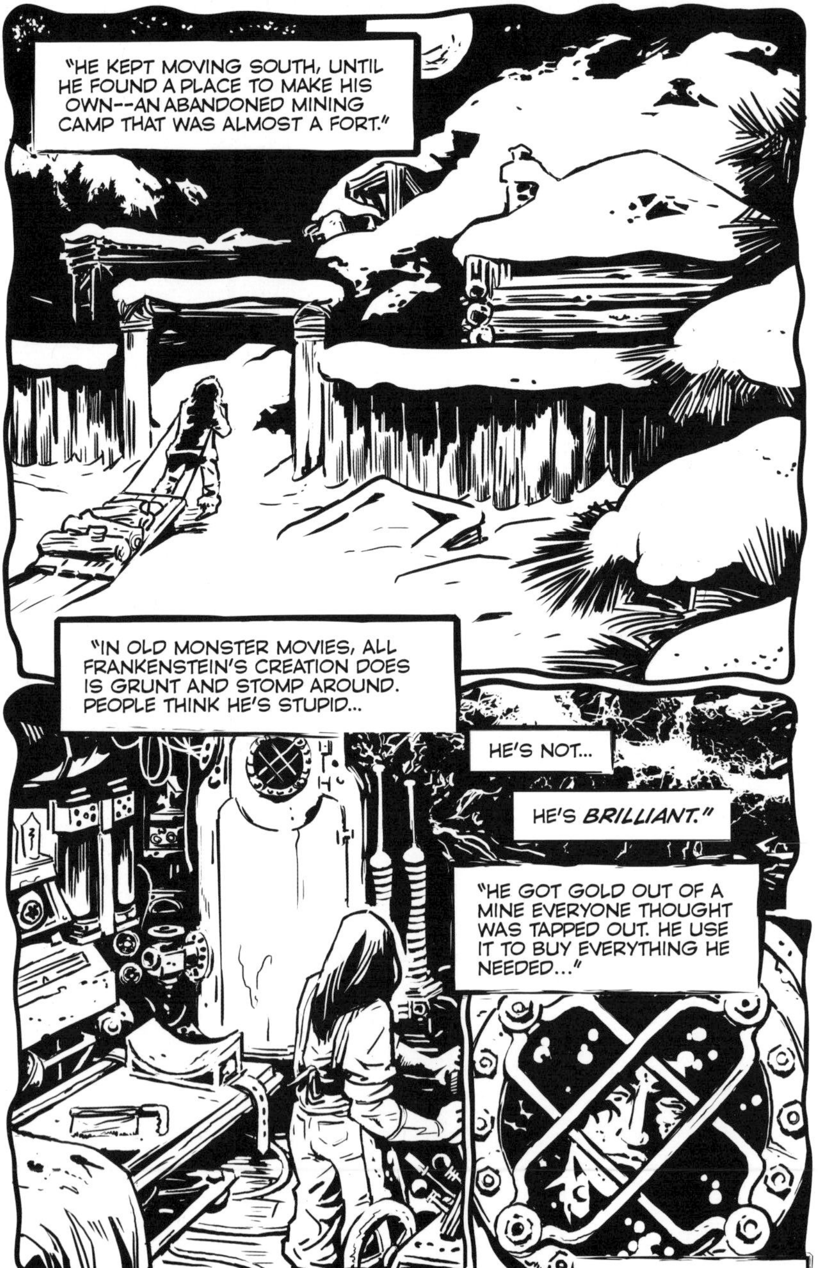
"HE KEPT MOVING SOUTH, UNTIL HE FOUND A PLACE TO MAKE HIS OWN--AN ABANDONED MINING CAMP THAT WAS ALMOST A FORT."
"IN OLD MONSTER MOVIES, ALL FRANKENSTEIN'S CREATION DOES IS GRUNT AND STOMP AROUND. PEOPLE THINK HE'S STUPID...
HE'S NOT...
HE'S *BRILLIANT.*"
"HE GOT GOLD OUT OF A MINE EVERYONE THOUGHT WAS TAPPED OUT. HE USE IT TO BUY EVERYTHING HE NEEDED..."
"...TO MAKE *ME!*"

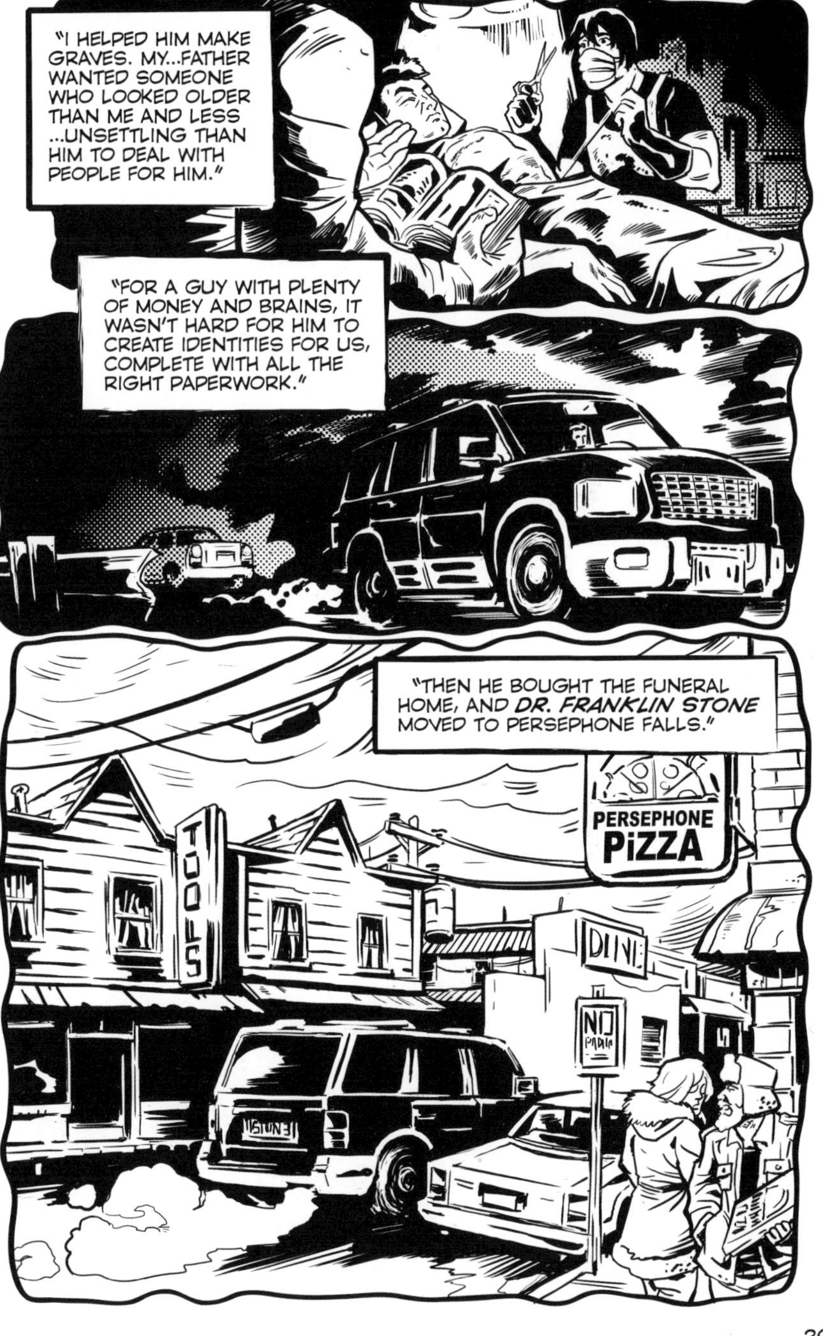
"I HELPED HIM MAKE GRAVES. MY...FATHER WANTED SOMEONE WHO LOOKED OLDER THAN ME AND LESS ...UNSETTLING THAN HIM TO DEAL WITH PEOPLE FOR HIM."
"FOR A GUY WITH PLENTY OF MONEY AND BRAINS, IT WASN'T HARD FOR HIM TO CREATE IDENTITIES FOR US, COMPLETE WITH ALL THE RIGHT PAPERWORK."
"THEN HE BOUGHT THE FUNERAL HOME, AND *DR. FRANKLIN STONE* MOVED TO PERSEPHONE FALLS."
PERSEPHONE PiZZA
TOOLS
STONE

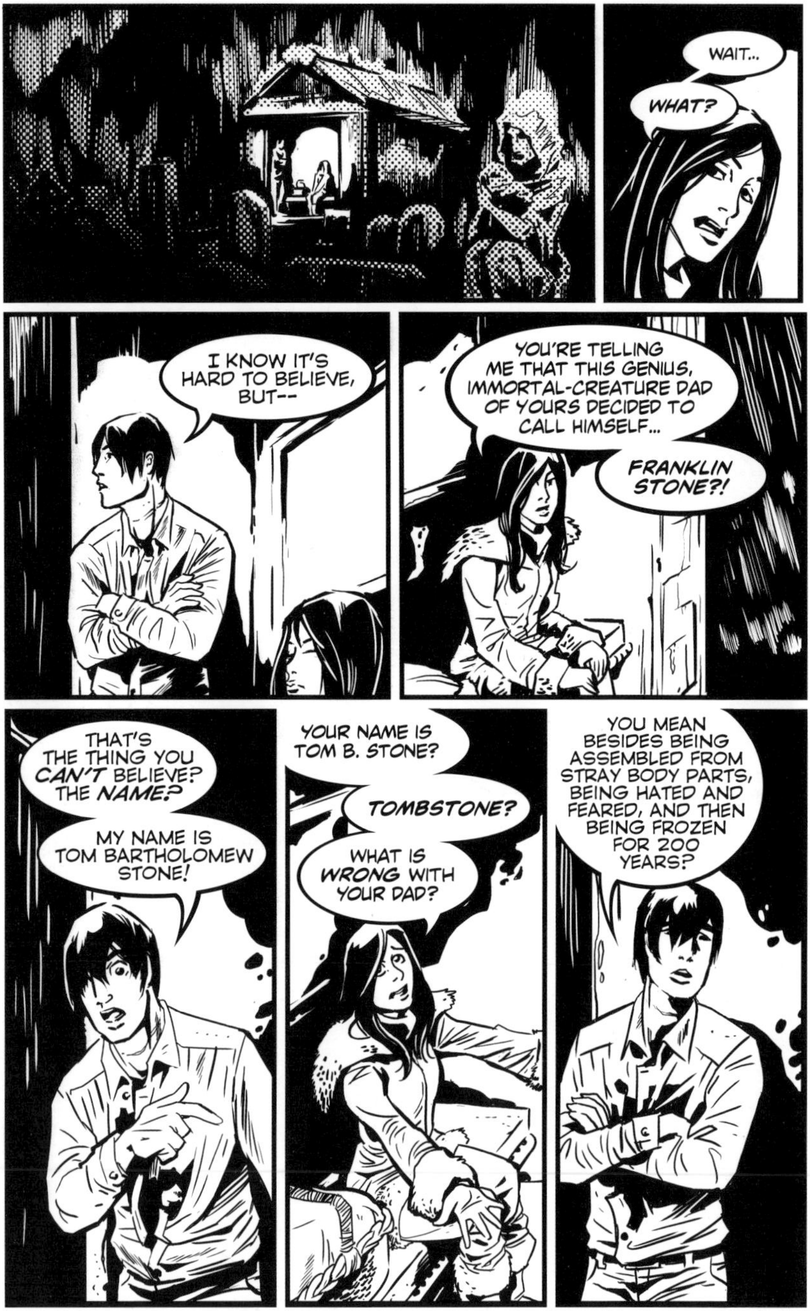
WAIT...
WHAT?
I KNOW IT'S HARD TO BELIEVE, BUT--
YOU'RE TELLING ME THAT THIS GENIUS, IMMORTAL-CREATURE DAD OF YOURS DECIDED TO CALL HIMSELF...
FRANKLIN STONE?!
THAT'S THE THING YOU CAN'T BELIEVE? THE NAME?
MY NAME IS TOM BARTHOLOMEW STONE!
YOUR NAME IS TOM B. STONE?
TOMBSTONE?
WHAT IS WRONG WITH YOUR DAD?
YOU MEAN BESIDES BEING ASSEMBLED FROM STRAY BODY PARTS, BEING HATED AND FEARED, AND THEN BEING FROZEN FOR 200 YEARS?

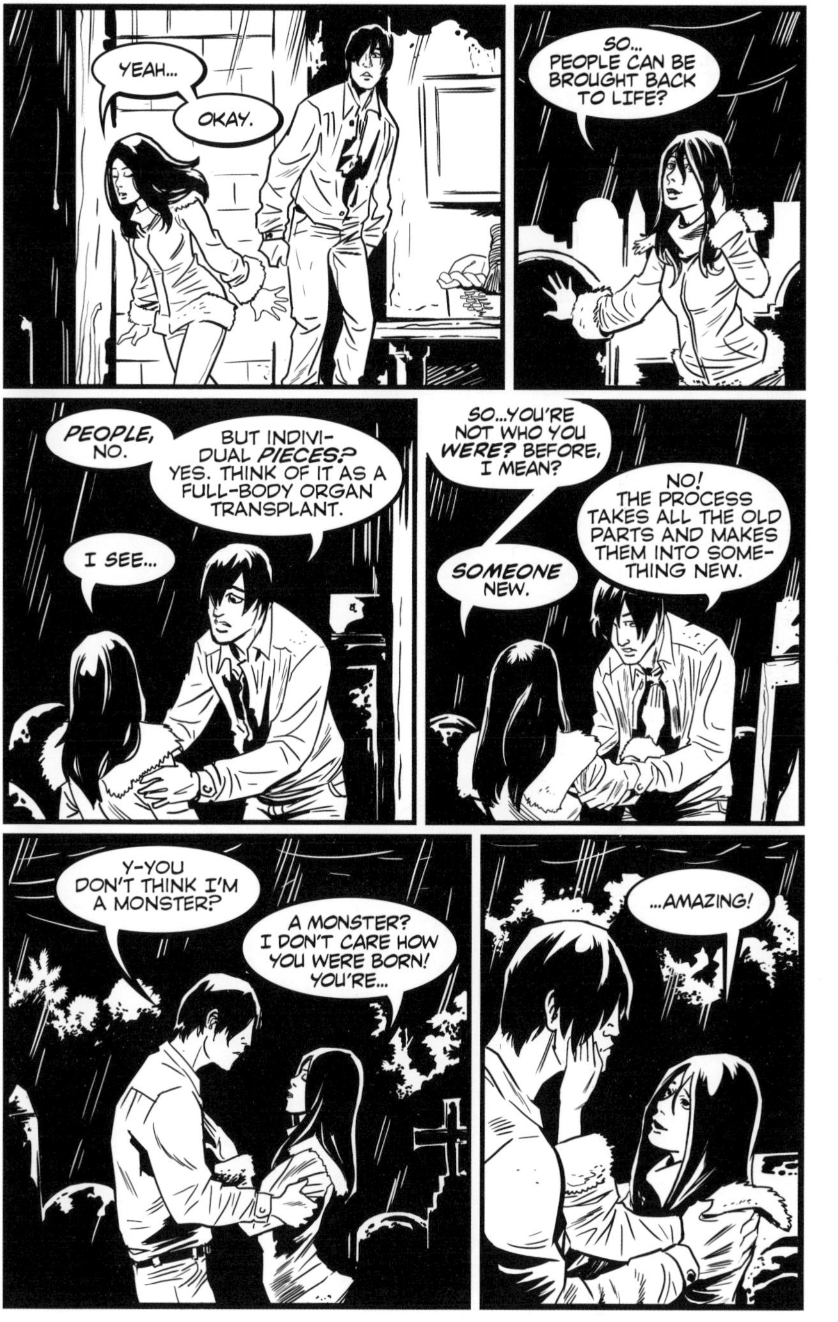
YEAH...
OKAY.
SO... PEOPLE CAN BE BROUGHT BACK TO LIFE?
PEOPLE, NO.
BUT INDIVIDUAL *PIECES?* YES. THINK OF IT AS A FULL-BODY ORGAN TRANSPLANT.
I SEE...
SO...YOU'RE NOT WHO YOU *WERE?* BEFORE, I MEAN?
NO! THE PROCESS TAKES ALL THE OLD PARTS AND MAKES THEM INTO SOMETHING NEW.
SOMEONE NEW.
Y-YOU DON'T THINK I'M A MONSTER?
A MONSTER? I DON'T CARE HOW YOU WERE BORN! YOU'RE...
...AMAZING!

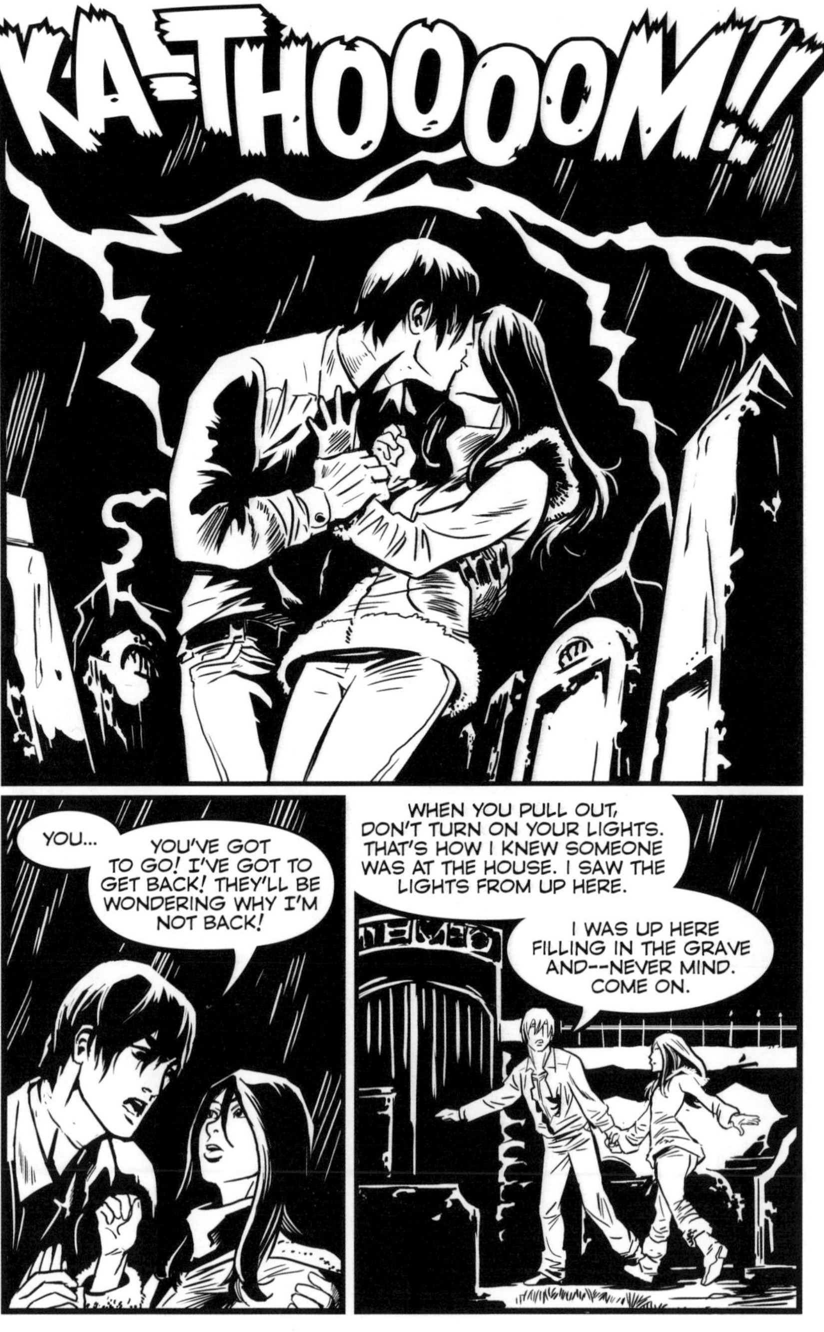
KA-THOOOOM!!
YOU...
YOU'VE GOT TO GO! I'VE GOT TO GET BACK! THEY'LL BE WONDERING WHY I'M NOT BACK!
WHEN YOU PULL OUT, DON'T TURN ON YOUR LIGHTS. THAT'S HOW I KNEW SOMEONE WAS AT THE HOUSE. I SAW THE LIGHTS FROM UP HERE.
I WAS UP HERE FILLING IN THE GRAVE AND--NEVER MIND. COME ON.

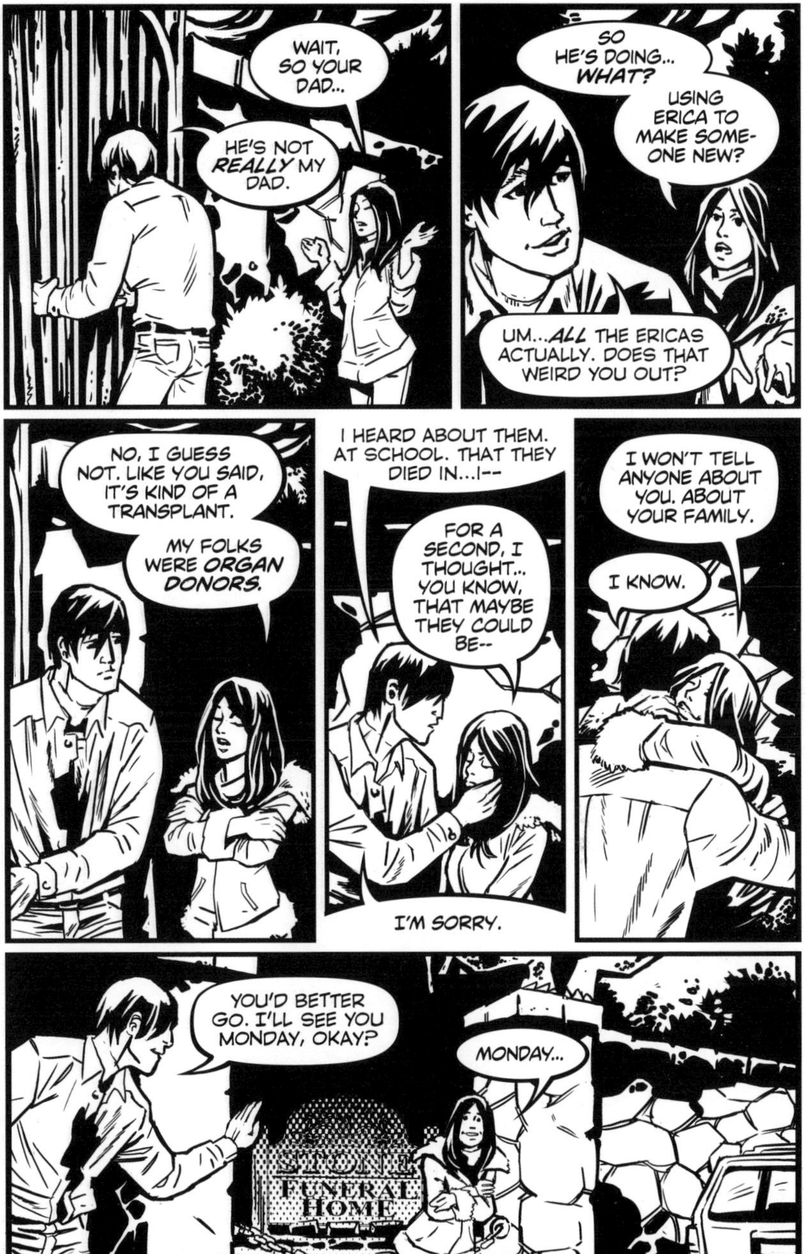
WAIT, SO YOUR DAD...
HE'S NOT REALLY MY DAD.
SO HE'S DOING... WHAT?
USING ERICA TO MAKE SOME-ONE NEW?
UM...ALL THE ERICAS ACTUALLY. DOES THAT WEIRD YOU OUT?
NO, I GUESS NOT. LIKE YOU SAID, IT'S KIND OF A TRANSPLANT.
MY FOLKS WERE ORGAN DONORS.
I HEARD ABOUT THEM. AT SCHOOL. THAT THEY DIED IN...I--
FOR A SECOND, I THOUGHT... YOU KNOW, THAT MAYBE THEY COULD BE--
I'M SORRY.
I WON'T TELL ANYONE ABOUT YOU. ABOUT YOUR FAMILY.
I KNOW.
YOU'D BETTER GO. I'LL SEE YOU MONDAY, OKAY?
MONDAY...
STONE FUNERAL HOME

44

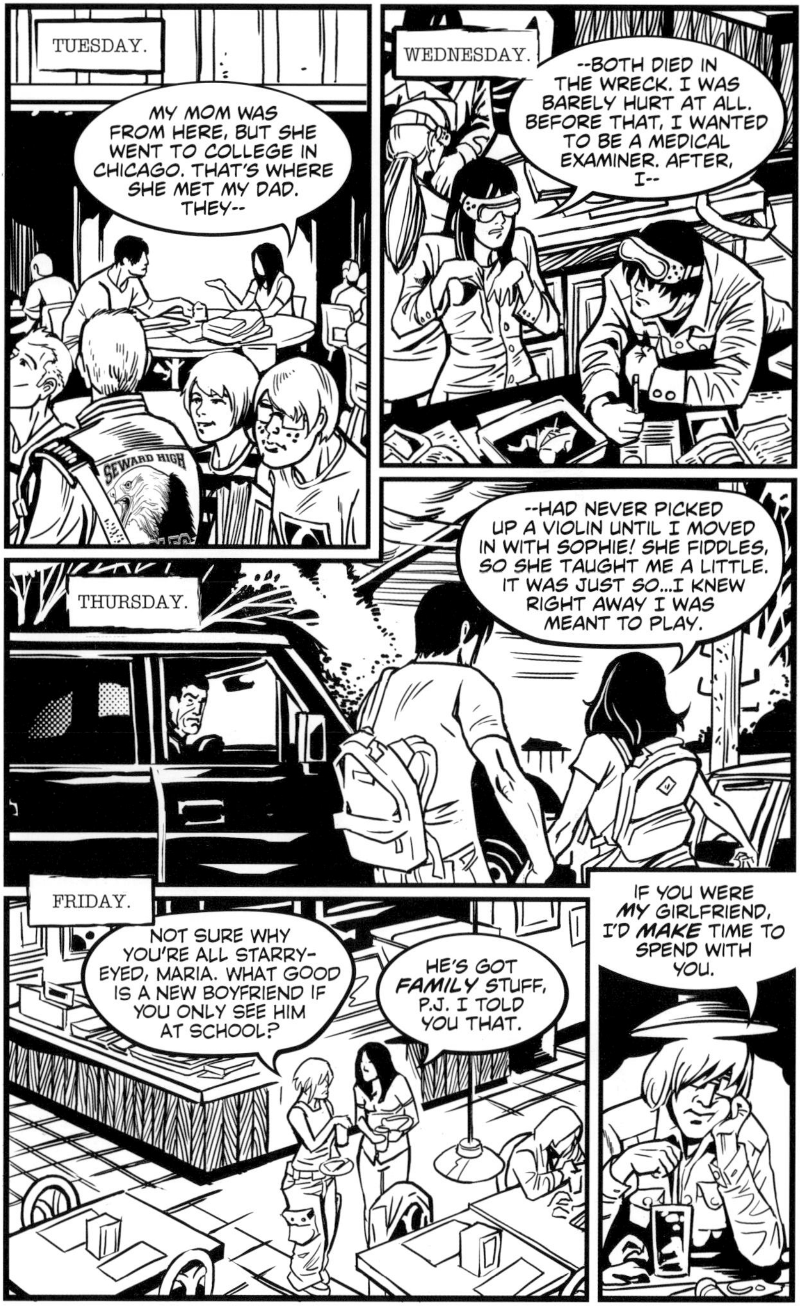
TUESDAY.
MY MOM WAS FROM HERE, BUT SHE WENT TO COLLEGE IN CHICAGO. THAT'S WHERE SHE MET MY DAD. THEY--
SEWARD HIGH
WEDNESDAY.
--BOTH DIED IN THE WRECK. I WAS BARELY HURT AT ALL. BEFORE THAT, I WANTED TO BE A MEDICAL EXAMINER. AFTER, I--
THURSDAY.
--HAD NEVER PICKED UP A VIOLIN UNTIL I MOVED IN WITH SOPHIE! SHE FIDDLES, SO SHE TAUGHT ME A LITTLE. IT WAS JUST SO...I KNEW RIGHT AWAY I WAS MEANT TO PLAY.
FRIDAY.
NOT SURE WHY YOU'RE ALL STARRY-EYED, MARIA. WHAT GOOD IS A NEW BOYFRIEND IF YOU ONLY SEE HIM AT SCHOOL?
HE'S GOT FAMILY STUFF, P.J. I TOLD YOU THAT.
IF YOU WERE MY GIRLFRIEND, I'D MAKE TIME TO SPEND WITH YOU.

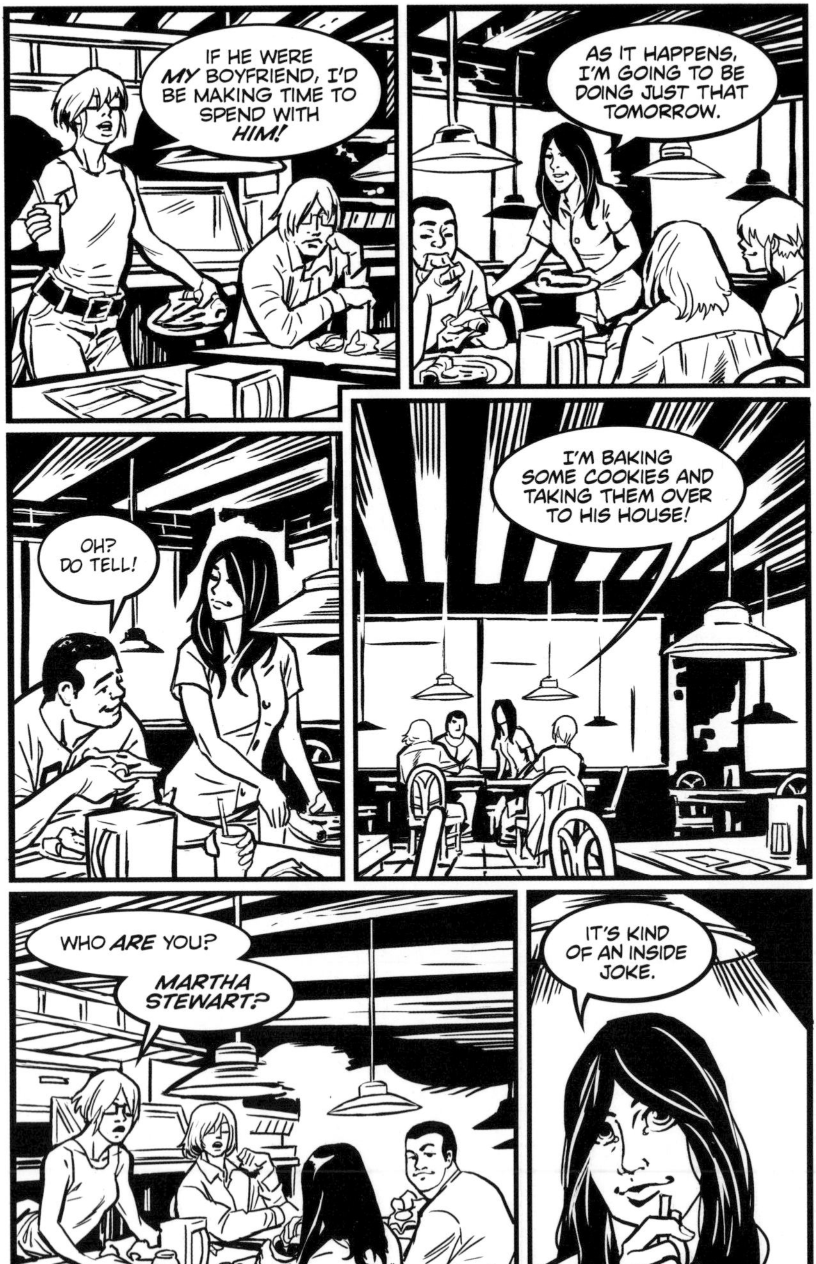

IF HE WERE *MY* BOYFRIEND, I'D BE MAKING TIME TO SPEND WITH *HIM!*
AS IT HAPPENS, I'M GOING TO BE DOING JUST THAT TOMORROW.
OH? DO TELL!
I'M BAKING SOME COOKIES AND TAKING THEM OVER TO HIS HOUSE!
WHO *ARE* YOU?
MARTHA STEWART?
IT'S KIND OF AN INSIDE JOKE.

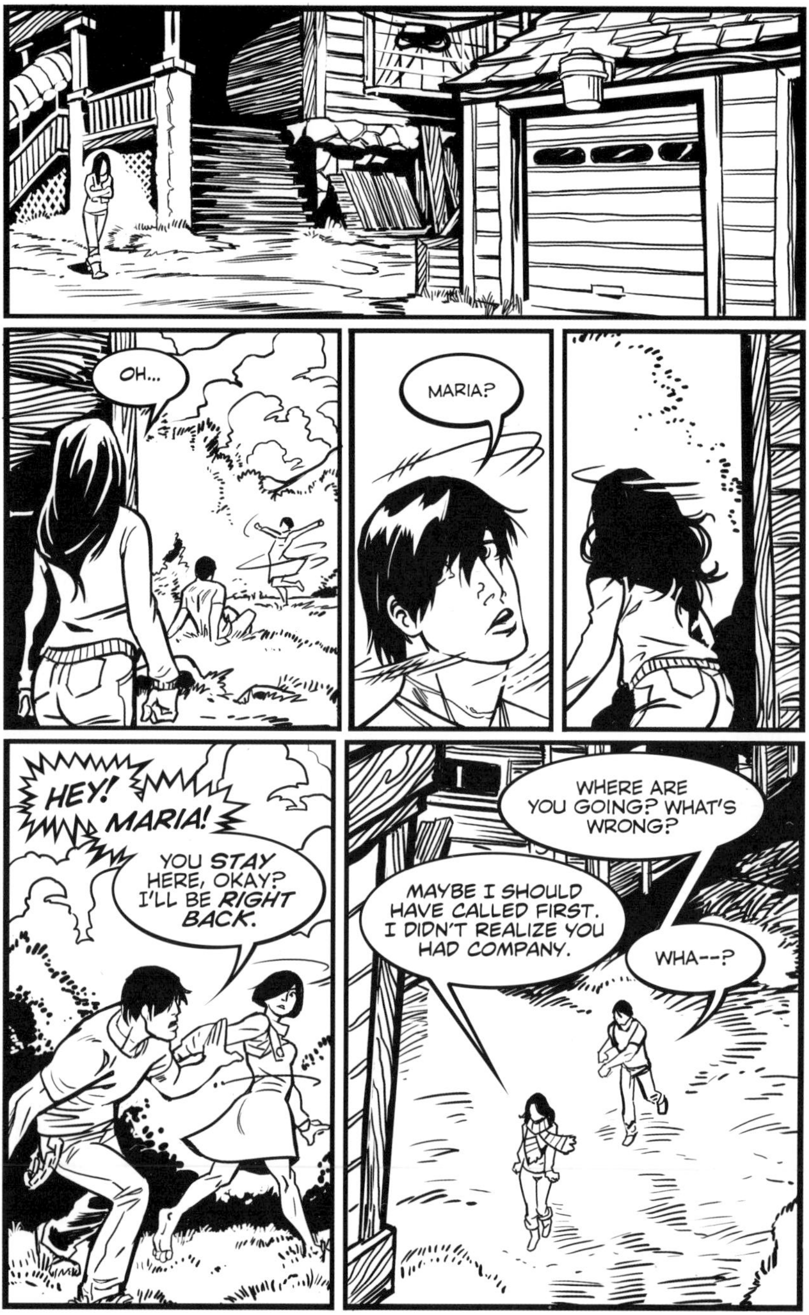
OH...
MARIA?
HEY! MARIA!
YOU STAY HERE, OKAY? I'LL BE RIGHT BACK.
WHERE ARE YOU GOING? WHAT'S WRONG?
MAYBE I SHOULD HAVE CALLED FIRST. I DIDN'T REALIZE YOU HAD COMPANY.
WHA--?

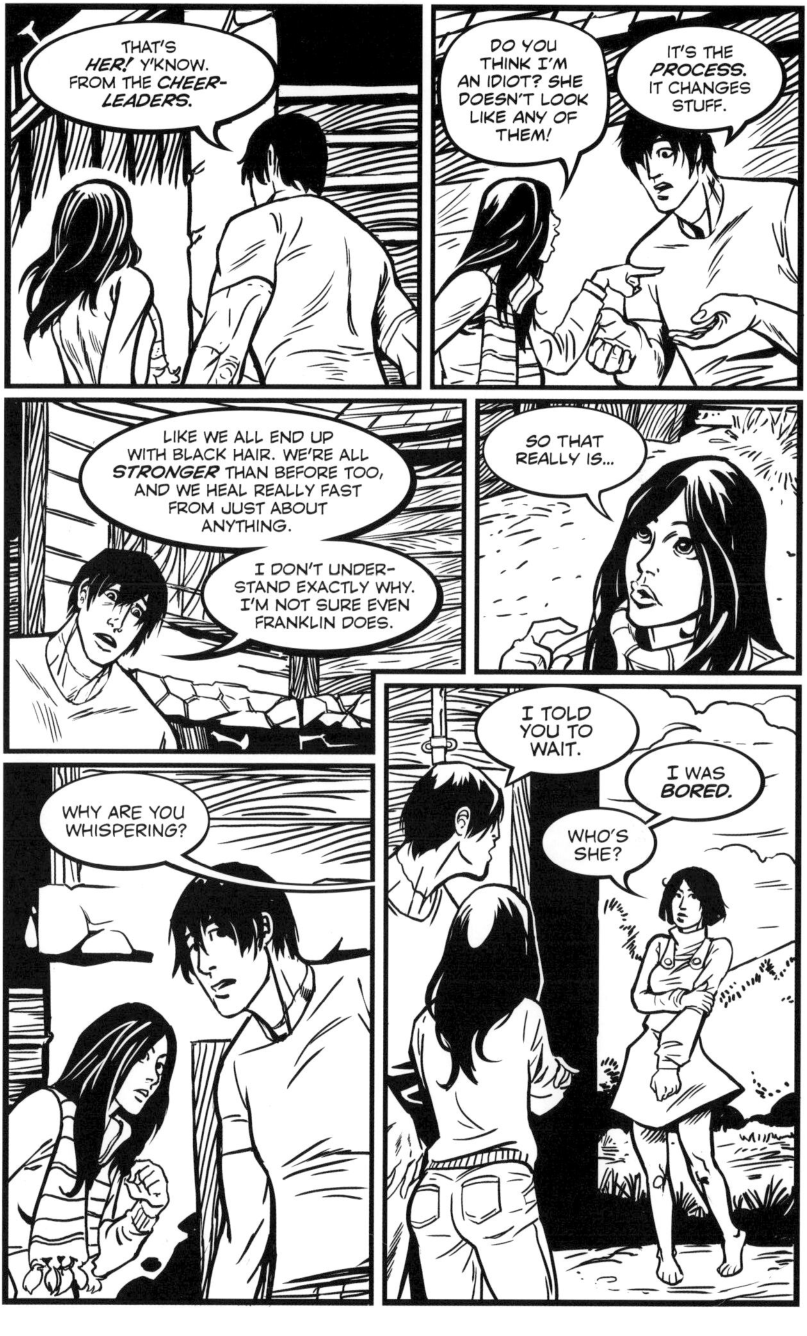
THAT'S *HER!* Y'KNOW. FROM THE *CHEER-LEADERS.*
DO YOU THINK I'M AN IDIOT? SHE DOESN'T LOOK LIKE ANY OF THEM!
IT'S THE *PROCESS.* IT CHANGES STUFF.
LIKE WE ALL END UP WITH BLACK HAIR. WE'RE ALL *STRONGER* THAN BEFORE TOO, AND WE HEAL REALLY FAST FROM JUST ABOUT ANYTHING.
I DON'T UNDER-STAND EXACTLY WHY. I'M NOT SURE EVEN FRANKLIN DOES.
SO THAT REALLY IS...
WHY ARE YOU WHISPERING?
I TOLD YOU TO WAIT.
I WAS *BORED.*
WHO'S SHE?

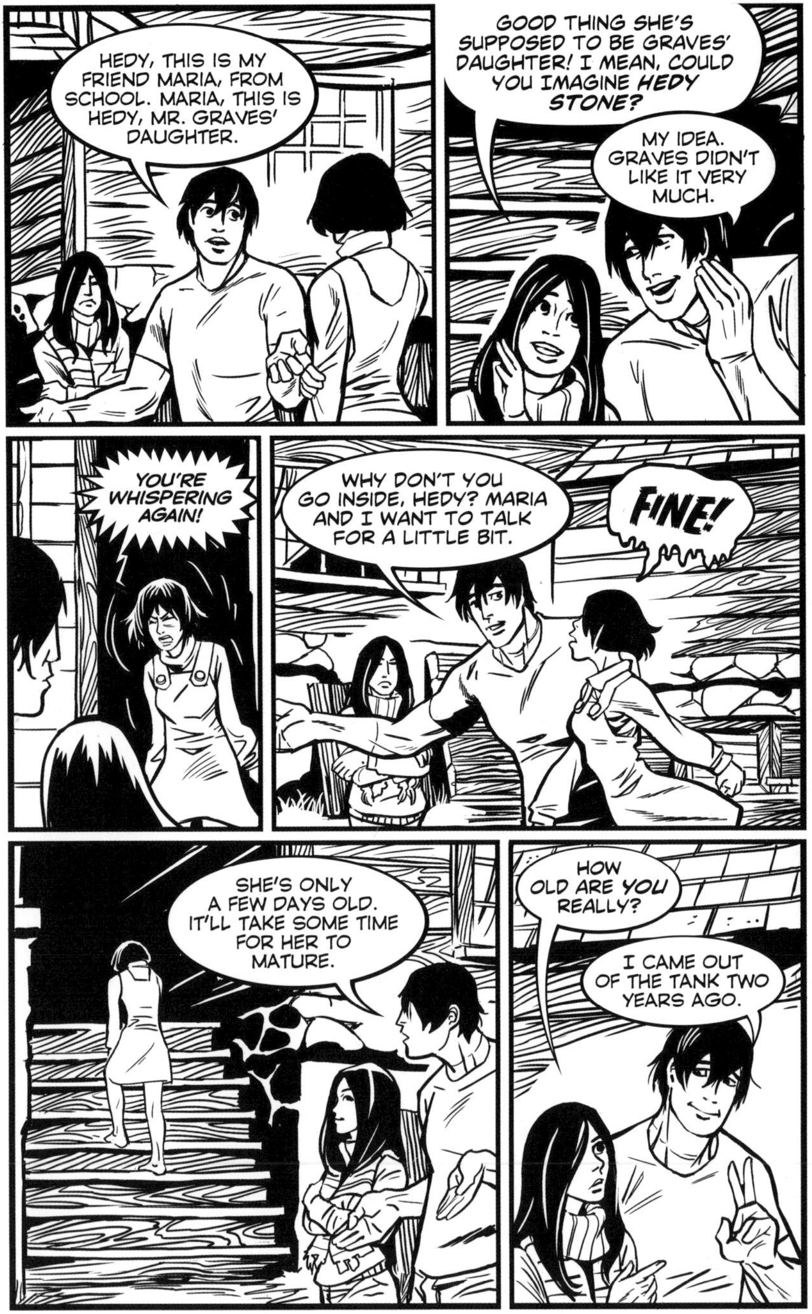
HEDY, THIS IS MY FRIEND MARIA, FROM SCHOOL. MARIA, THIS IS HEDY, MR. GRAVES' DAUGHTER.
GOOD THING SHE'S SUPPOSED TO BE GRAVES' DAUGHTER! I MEAN, COULD YOU IMAGINE *HEDY STONE?*
MY IDEA. GRAVES DIDN'T LIKE IT VERY MUCH.
YOU'RE WHISPERING AGAIN!
WHY DON'T YOU GO INSIDE, HEDY? MARIA AND I WANT TO TALK FOR A LITTLE BIT.
FINE!
SHE'S ONLY A FEW DAYS OLD. IT'LL TAKE SOME TIME FOR HER TO MATURE.
HOW OLD ARE *YOU* REALLY?
I CAME OUT OF THE TANK TWO YEARS AGO.

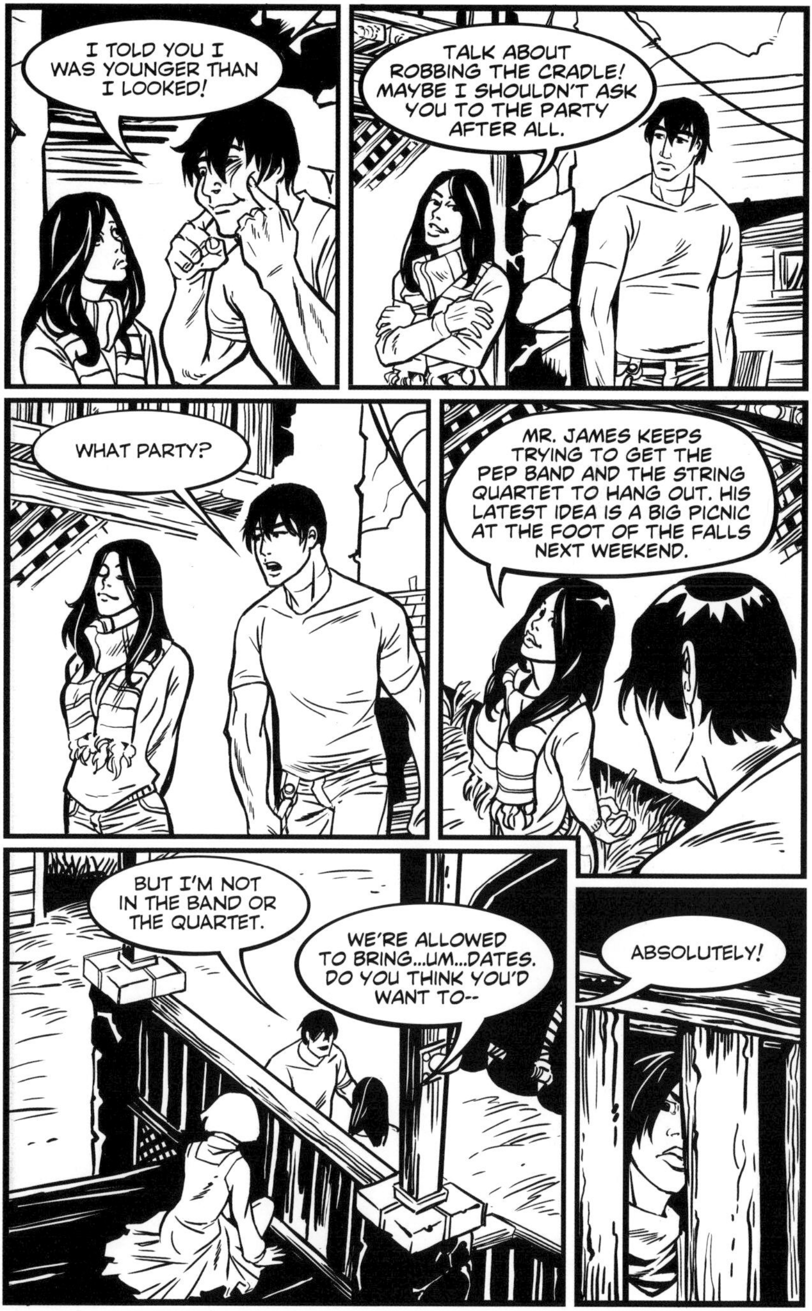
I TOLD YOU I WAS YOUNGER THAN I LOOKED!
TALK ABOUT ROBBING THE CRADLE! MAYBE I SHOULDN'T ASK YOU TO THE PARTY AFTER ALL.
WHAT PARTY?
MR. JAMES KEEPS TRYING TO GET THE PEP BAND AND THE STRING QUARTET TO HANG OUT. HIS LATEST IDEA IS A BIG PICNIC AT THE FOOT OF THE FALLS NEXT WEEKEND.
BUT I'M NOT IN THE BAND OR THE QUARTET.
WE'RE ALLOWED TO BRING...UM...DATES. DO YOU THINK YOU'D WANT TO--
ABSOLUTELY!

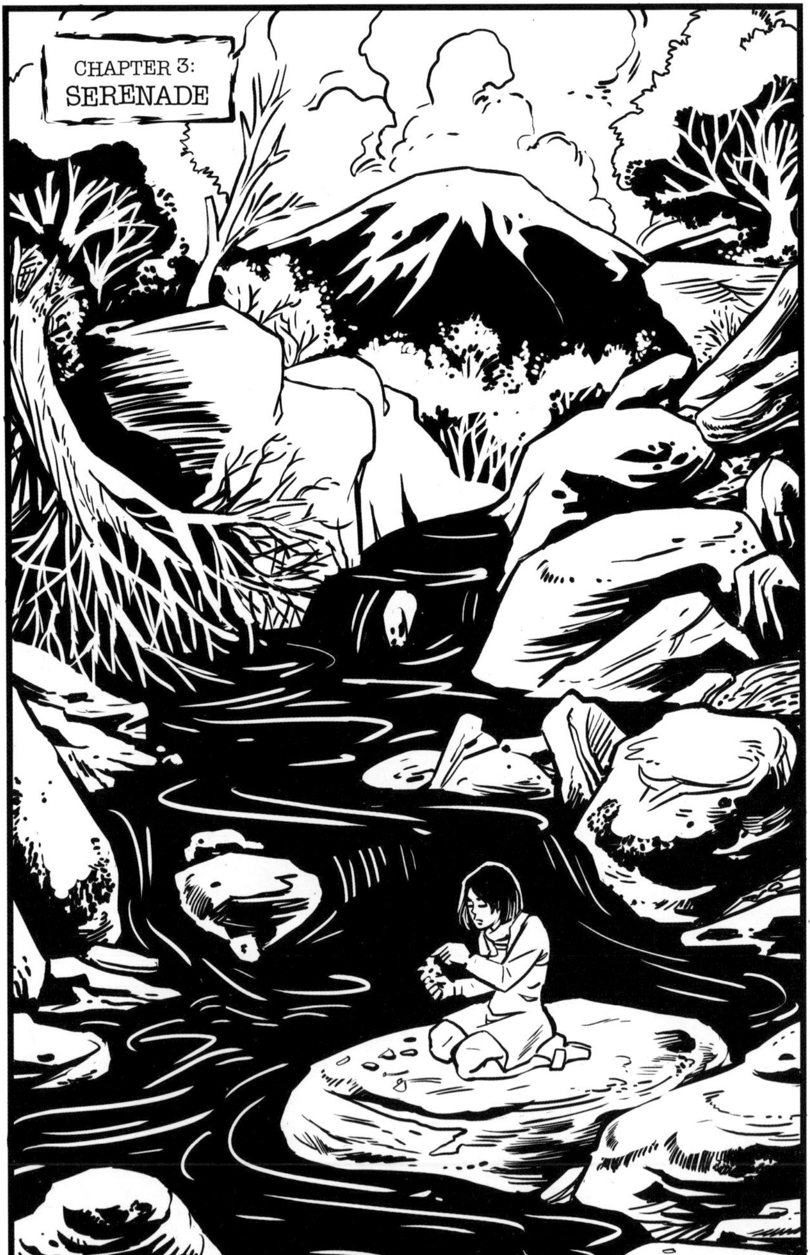
CHAPTER 3:
SERENADE

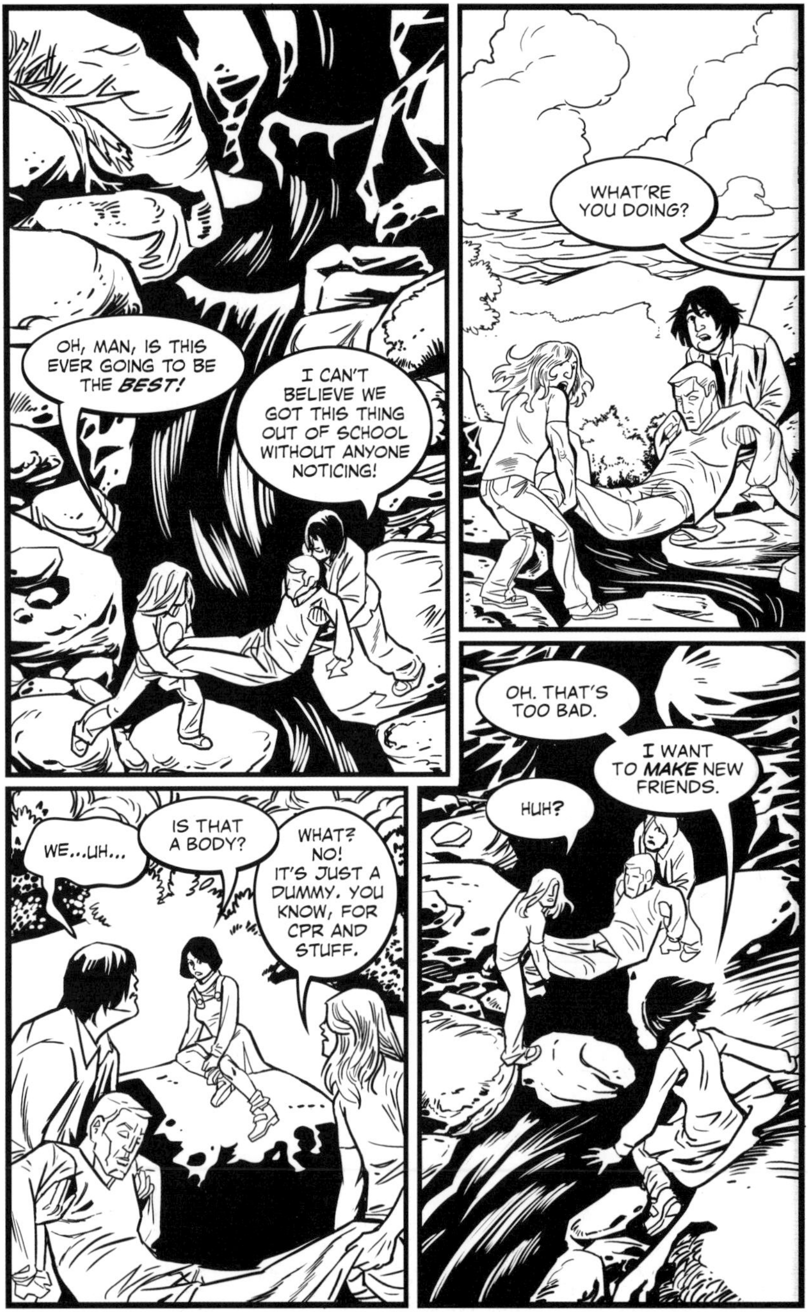
OH, MAN, IS THIS EVER GOING TO BE THE *BEST!*
I CAN'T BELIEVE WE GOT THIS THING OUT OF SCHOOL WITHOUT ANYONE NOTICING!
WHAT'RE YOU DOING?
WE...UH...
IS THAT A BODY?
WHAT? NO! IT'S JUST A DUMMY. YOU KNOW, FOR CPR AND STUFF.
OH. THAT'S TOO BAD.
I WANT TO *MAKE* NEW FRIENDS.
HUH?

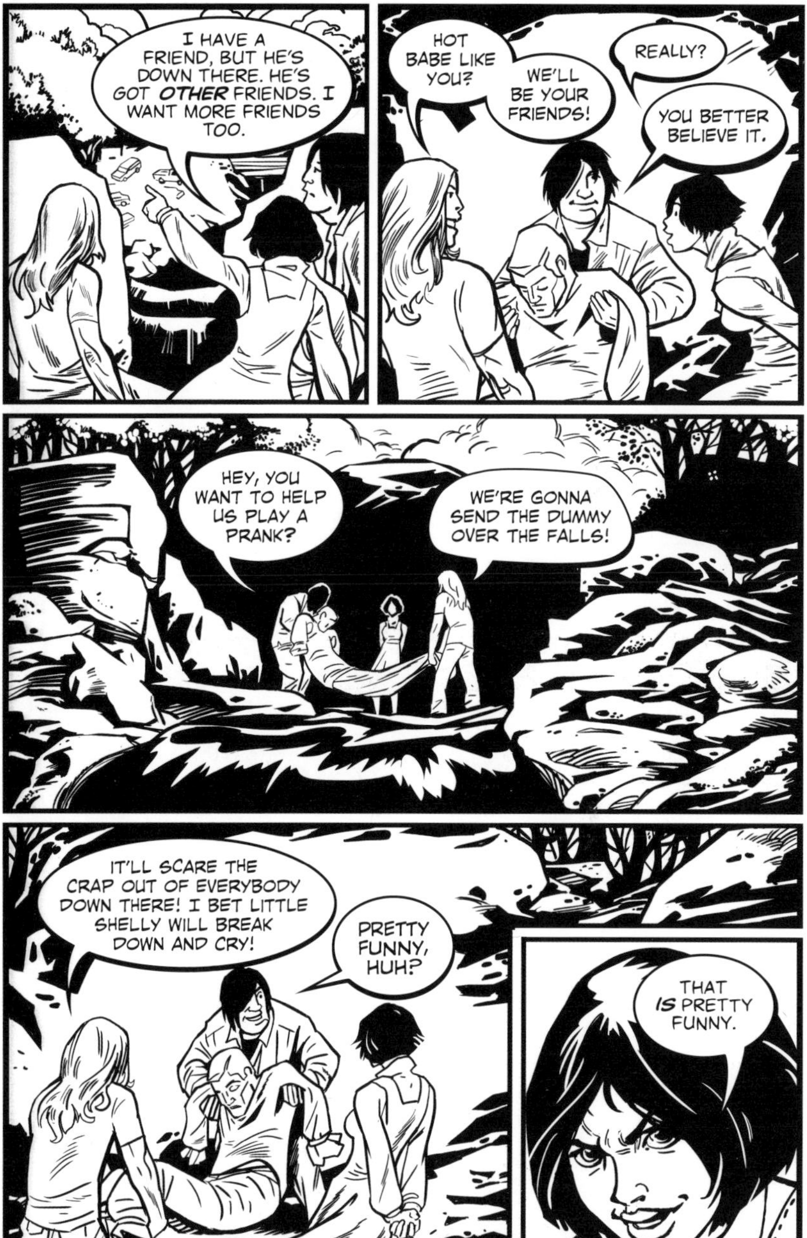
I HAVE A FRIEND, BUT HE'S DOWN THERE. HE'S GOT OTHER FRIENDS. I WANT MORE FRIENDS TOO.
HOT BABE LIKE YOU?
WE'LL BE YOUR FRIENDS!
REALLY?
YOU BETTER BELIEVE IT.
HEY, YOU WANT TO HELP US PLAY A PRANK?
WE'RE GONNA SEND THE DUMMY OVER THE FALLS!
IT'LL SCARE THE CRAP OUT OF EVERYBODY DOWN THERE! I BET LITTLE SHELLY WILL BREAK DOWN AND CRY!
PRETTY FUNNY, HUH?
THAT IS PRETTY FUNNY.

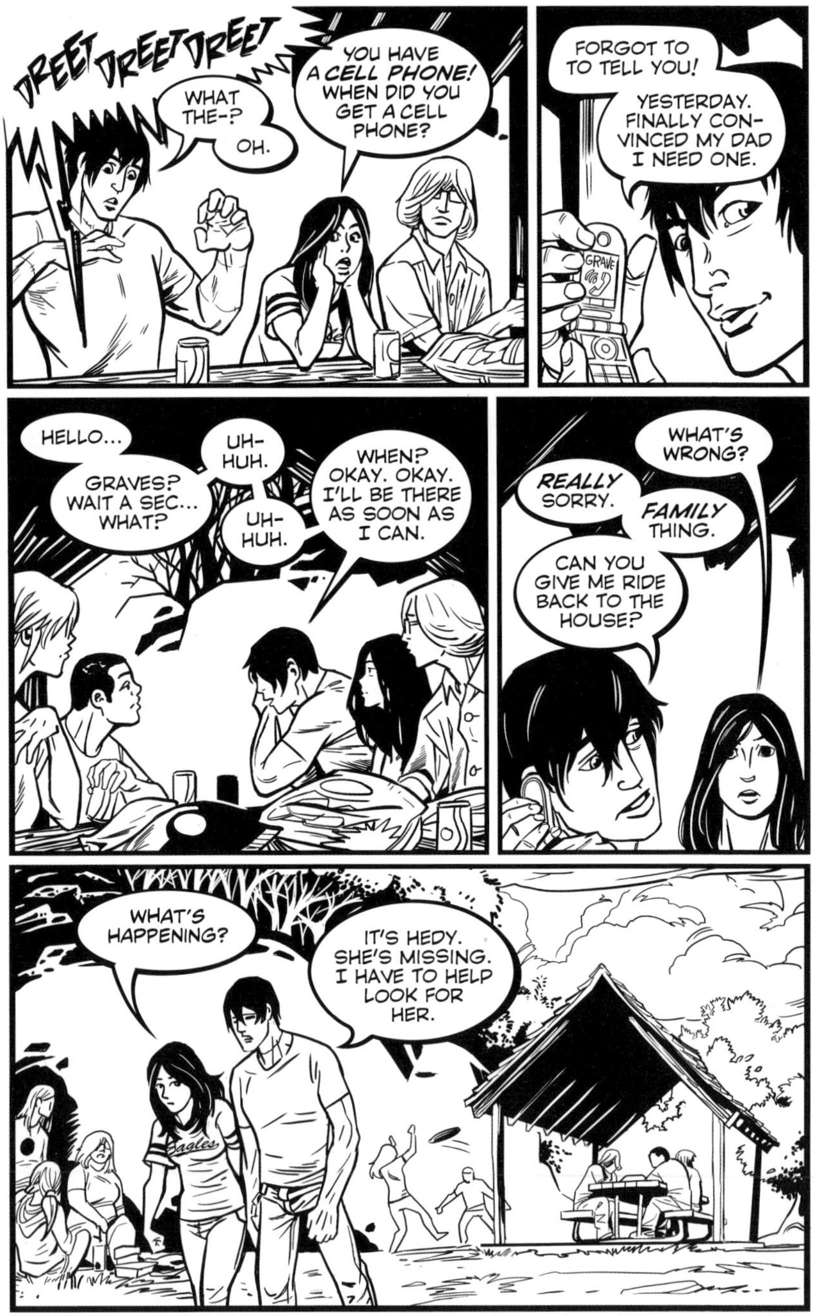
DREET DREET DREET
WHAT THE-?
OH.
YOU HAVE A CELL PHONE! WHEN DID YOU GET A CELL PHONE?
FORGOT TO TO TELL YOU!
YESTERDAY. FINALLY CON- VINCED MY DAD I NEED ONE.
GRAVE
HELLO...
GRAVES? WAIT A SEC... WHAT?
UH- HUH.
UH- HUH.
WHEN? OKAY. OKAY. I'LL BE THERE AS SOON AS I CAN.
REALLY SORRY.
FAMILY THING.
WHAT'S WRONG?
CAN YOU GIVE ME RIDE BACK TO THE HOUSE?
WHAT'S HAPPENING?
IT'S HEDY. SHE'S MISSING. I HAVE TO HELP LOOK FOR HER.
Eagles

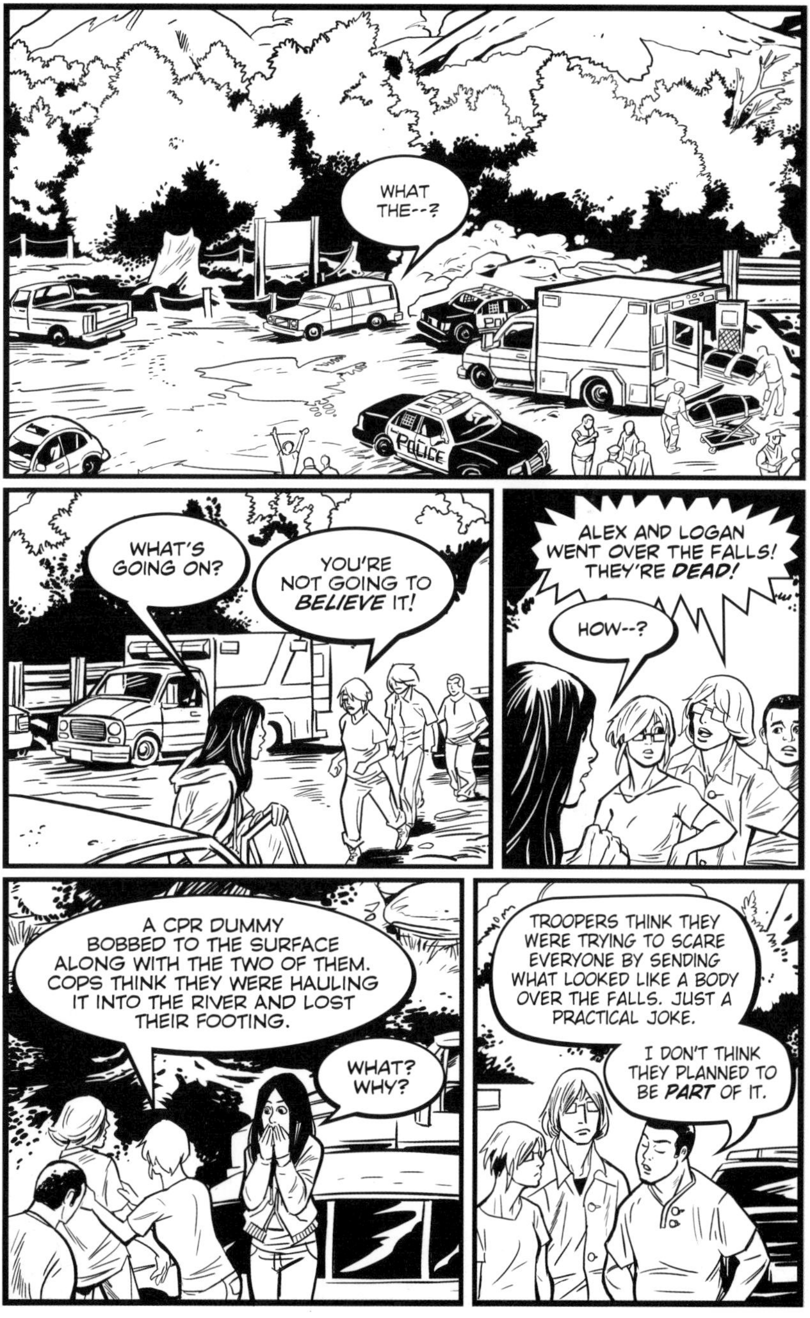
WHAT THE--?
WHAT'S GOING ON?
YOU'RE NOT GOING TO *BELIEVE* IT!
ALEX AND LOGAN WENT OVER THE FALLS! THEY'RE *DEAD!*
HOW--?
A CPR DUMMY BOBBED TO THE SURFACE ALONG WITH THE TWO OF THEM. COPS THINK THEY WERE HAULING IT INTO THE RIVER AND LOST THEIR FOOTING.
WHAT? WHY?
TROOPERS THINK THEY WERE TRYING TO SCARE EVERYONE BY SENDING WHAT LOOKED LIKE A BODY OVER THE FALLS. JUST A PRACTICAL JOKE.
I DON'T THINK THEY PLANNED TO BE *PART* OF IT.
POLICE

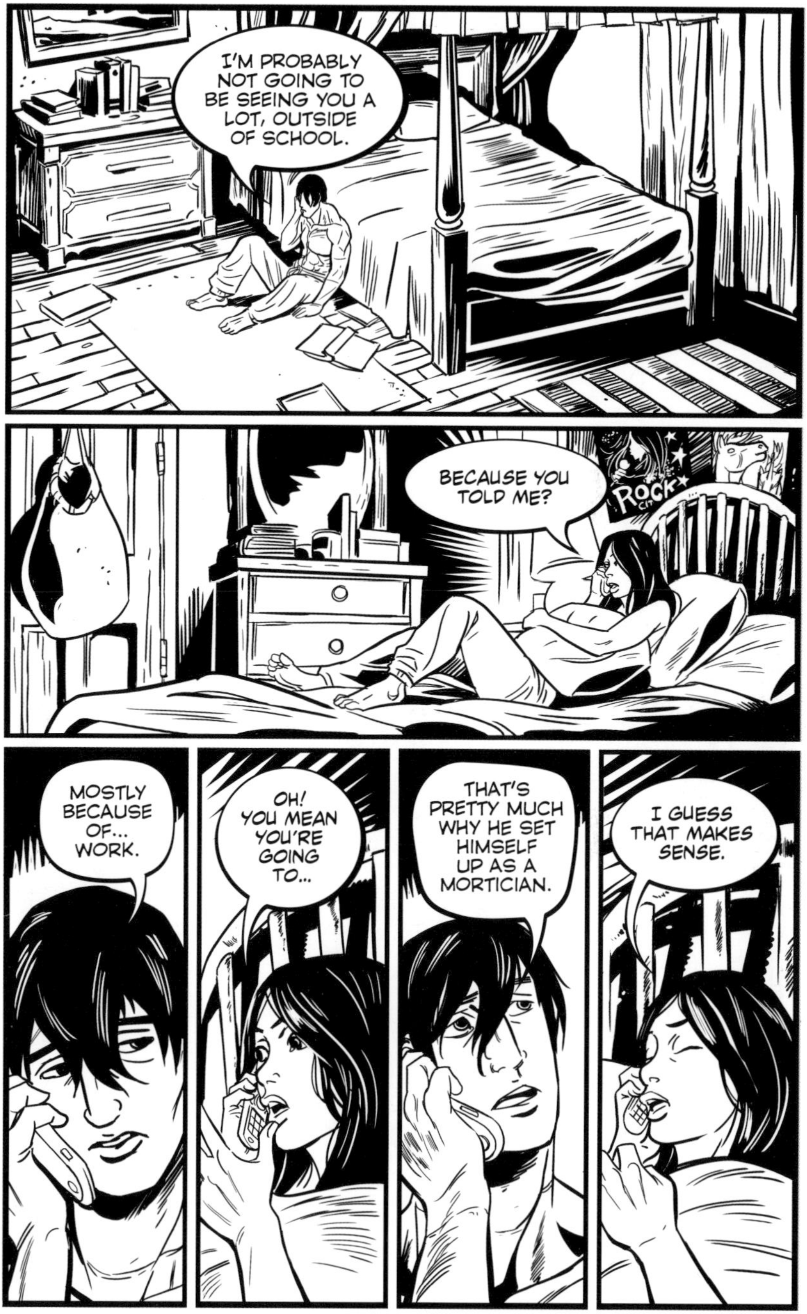
I'M PROBABLY NOT GOING TO BE SEEING YOU A LOT, OUTSIDE OF SCHOOL.
BECAUSE YOU TOLD ME?
ROCK
MOSTLY BECAUSE OF... WORK.
OH! YOU MEAN YOU'RE GOING TO...
THAT'S PRETTY MUCH WHY HE SET HIMSELF UP AS A MORTICIAN.
I GUESS THAT MAKES SENSE.

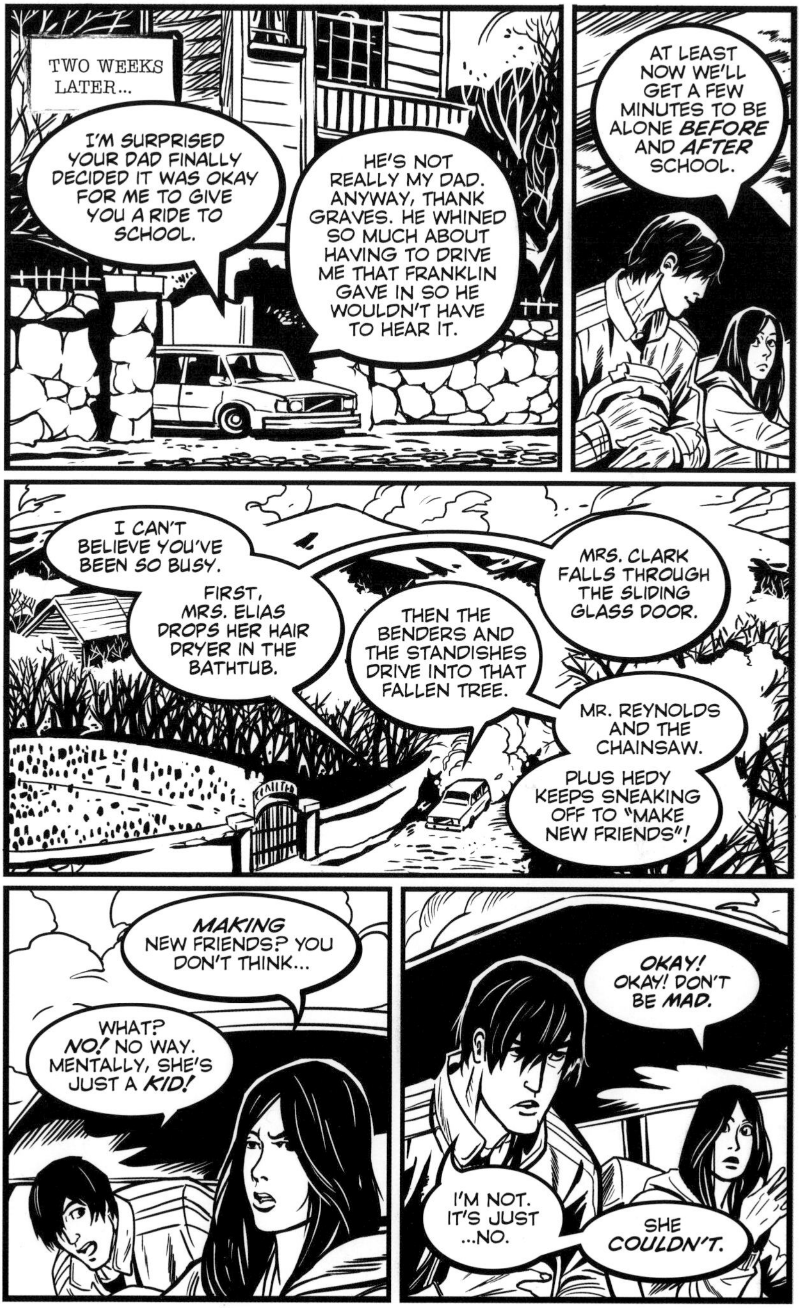
TWO WEEKS LATER...
I'M SURPRISED YOUR DAD FINALLY DECIDED IT WAS OKAY FOR ME TO GIVE YOU A RIDE TO SCHOOL.
HE'S NOT REALLY MY DAD. ANYWAY, THANK GRAVES. HE WHINED SO MUCH ABOUT HAVING TO DRIVE ME THAT FRANKLIN GAVE IN SO HE WOULDN'T HAVE TO HEAR IT.
AT LEAST NOW WE'LL GET A FEW MINUTES TO BE ALONE *BEFORE* AND *AFTER* SCHOOL.
I CAN'T BELIEVE YOU'VE BEEN SO BUSY.
FIRST, MRS. ELIAS DROPS HER HAIR DRYER IN THE BATHTUB.
THEN THE BENDERS AND THE STANDISHES DRIVE INTO THAT FALLEN TREE.
MRS. CLARK FALLS THROUGH THE SLIDING GLASS DOOR.
MR. REYNOLDS AND THE CHAINSAW.
PLUS HEDY KEEPS SNEAKING OFF TO "MAKE NEW FRIENDS"!
MAKING NEW FRIENDS? YOU DON'T THINK...
WHAT? *NO!* NO WAY. MENTALLY, SHE'S JUST A *KID!*
OKAY! OKAY! DON'T BE *MAD.*
I'M NOT. IT'S JUST ...NO.
SHE *COULDN'T.*

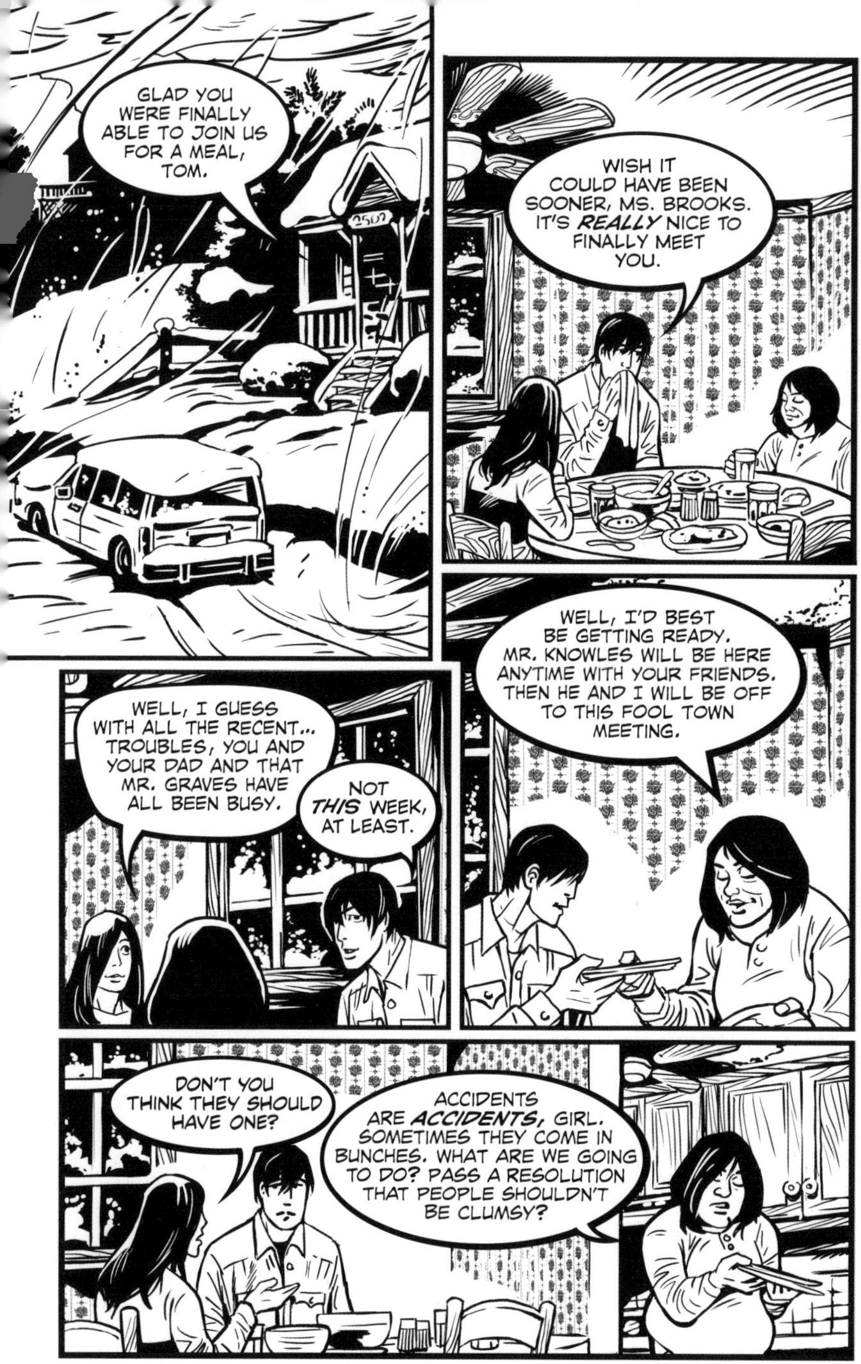
GLAD YOU WERE FINALLY ABLE TO JOIN US FOR A MEAL, TOM.
2507
WISH IT COULD HAVE BEEN SOONER, MS. BROOKS. IT'S *REALLY* NICE TO FINALLY MEET YOU.
WELL, I GUESS WITH ALL THE RECENT... TROUBLES, YOU AND YOUR DAD AND THAT MR. GRAVES HAVE ALL BEEN BUSY.
NOT *THIS* WEEK, AT LEAST.
WELL, I'D BEST BE GETTING READY. MR. KNOWLES WILL BE HERE ANYTIME WITH YOUR FRIENDS. THEN HE AND I WILL BE OFF TO THIS FOOL TOWN MEETING.
DON'T YOU THINK THEY SHOULD HAVE ONE?
ACCIDENTS ARE *ACCIDENTS,* GIRL. SOMETIMES THEY COME IN BUNCHES. WHAT ARE WE GOING TO DO? PASS A RESOLUTION THAT PEOPLE SHOULDN'T BE CLUMSY?

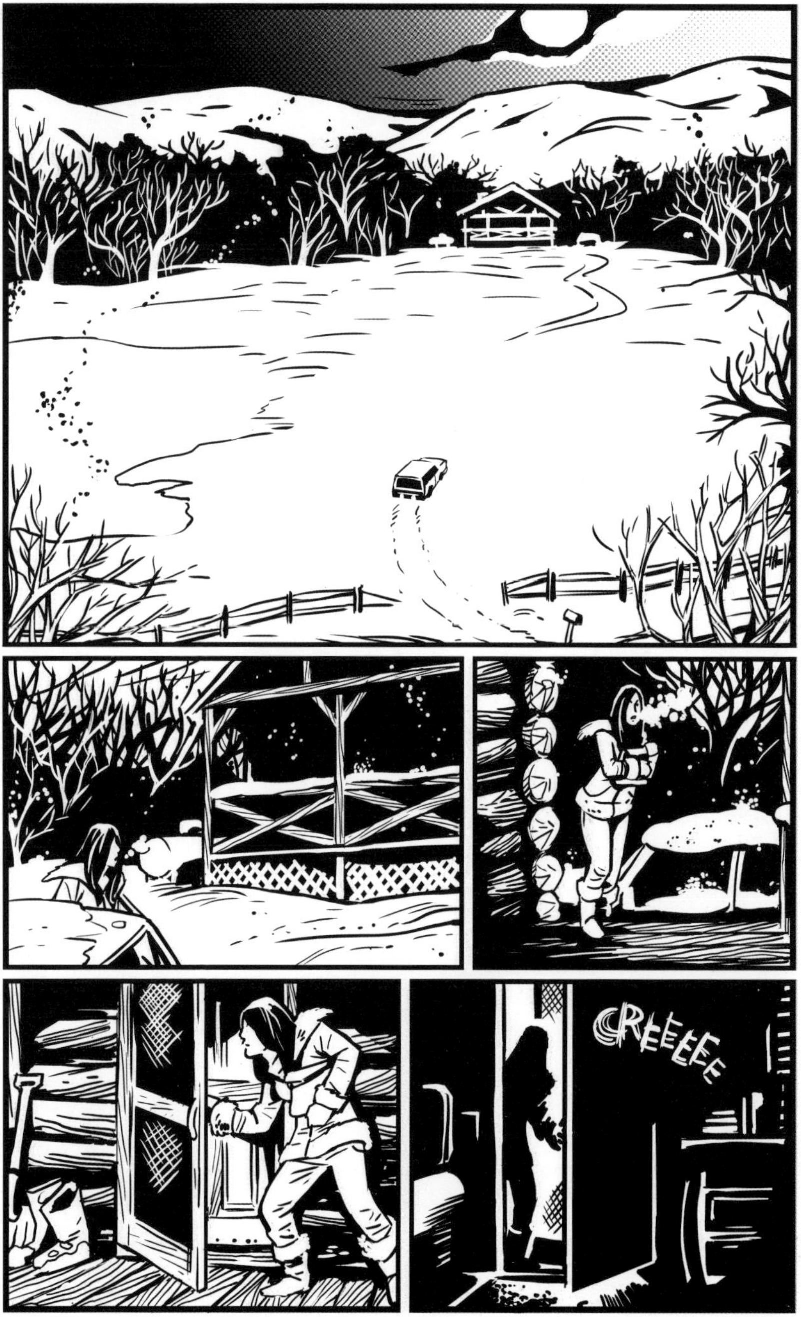
CREEEEE

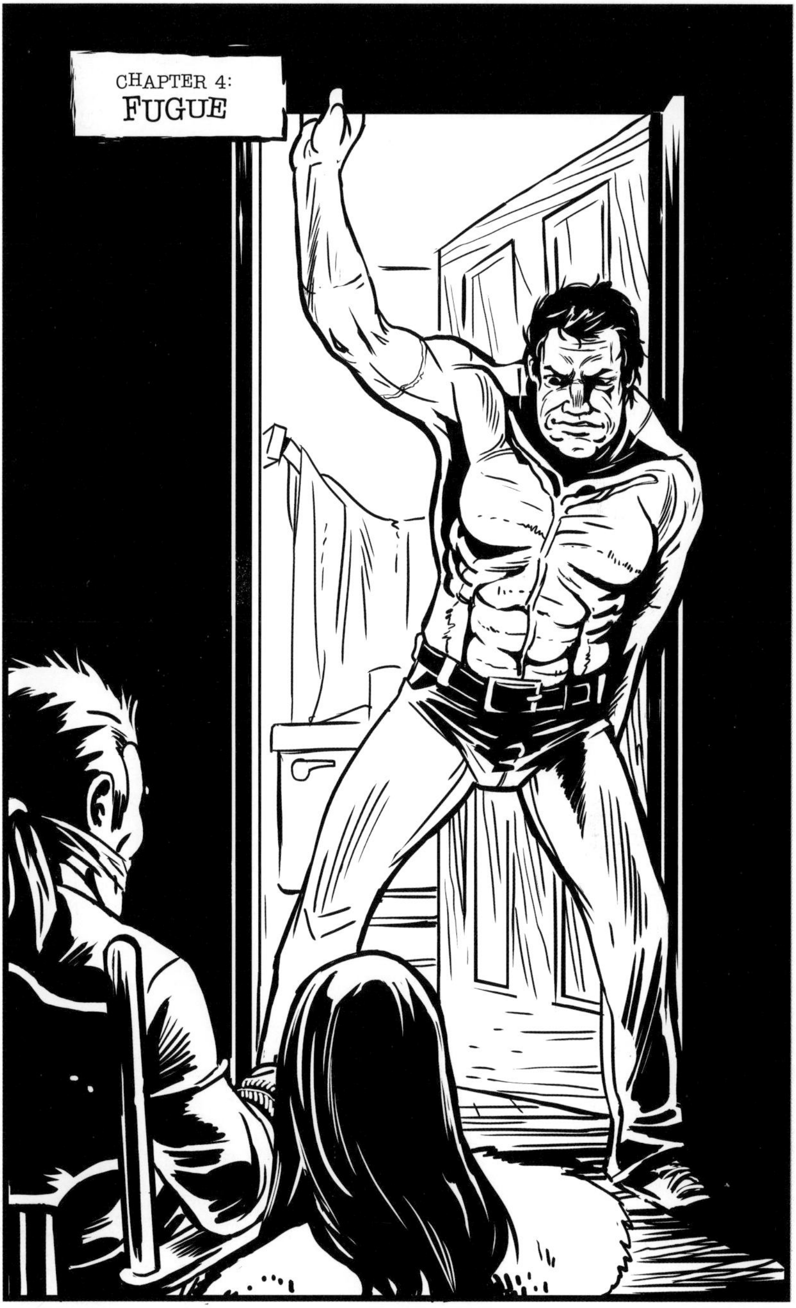
CHAPTER 4:
FUGUE

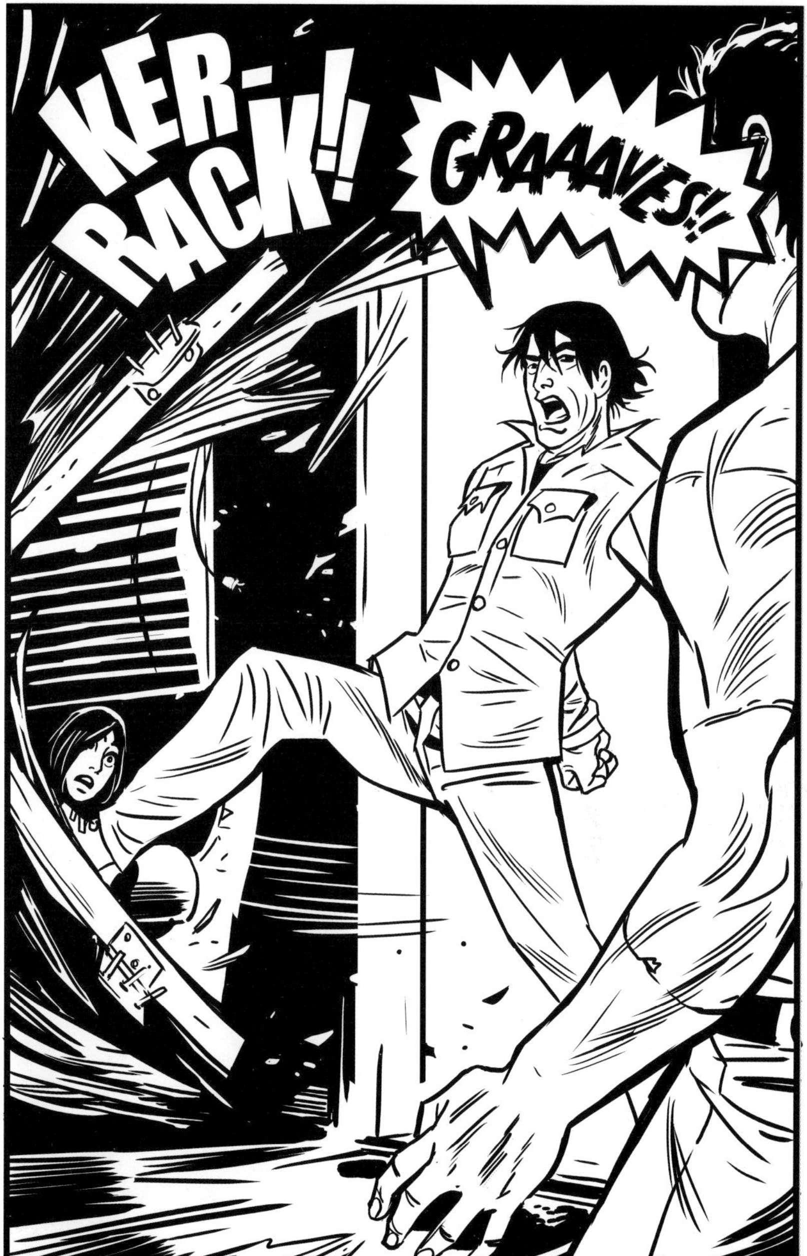
KER-RACK!!
GRAAAVES!!

86

92

94

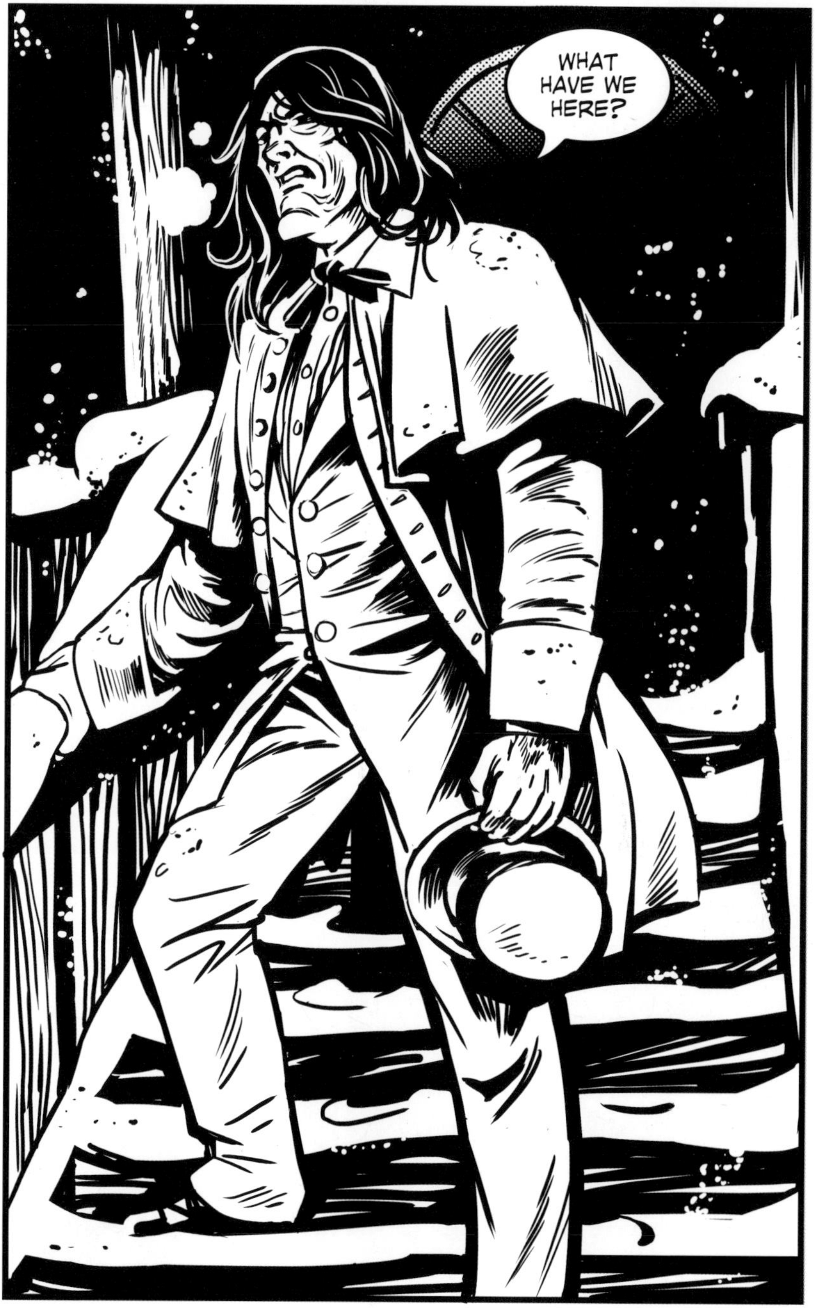
WHAT HAVE WE HERE?

98

99

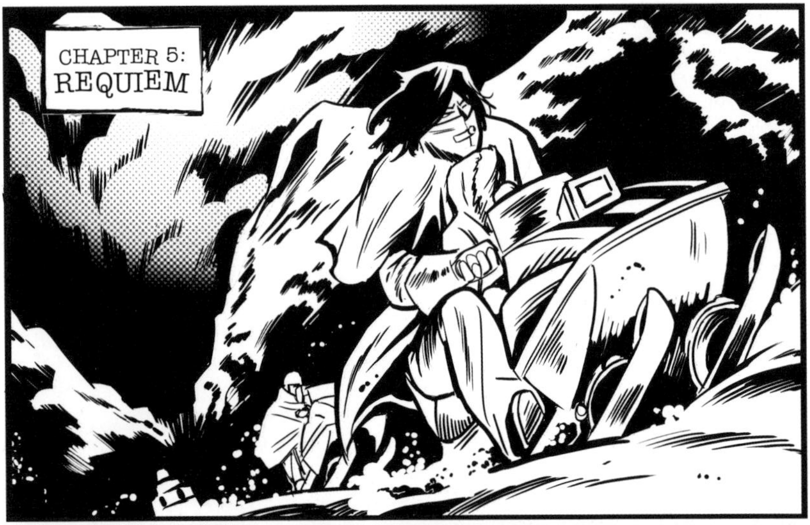
CHAPTER 5:
REQUIEM

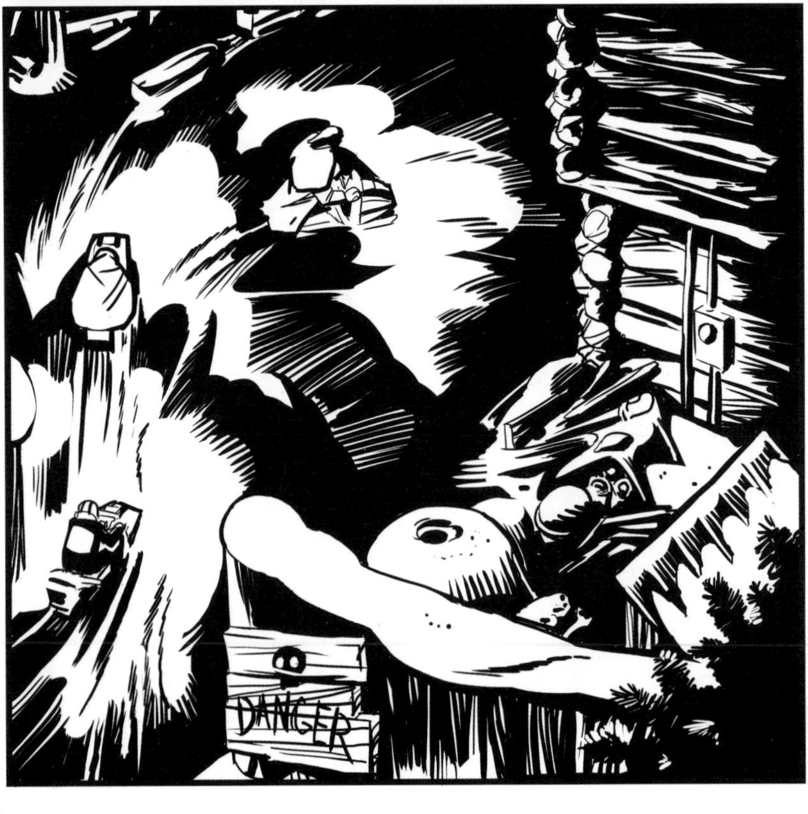
DANGER

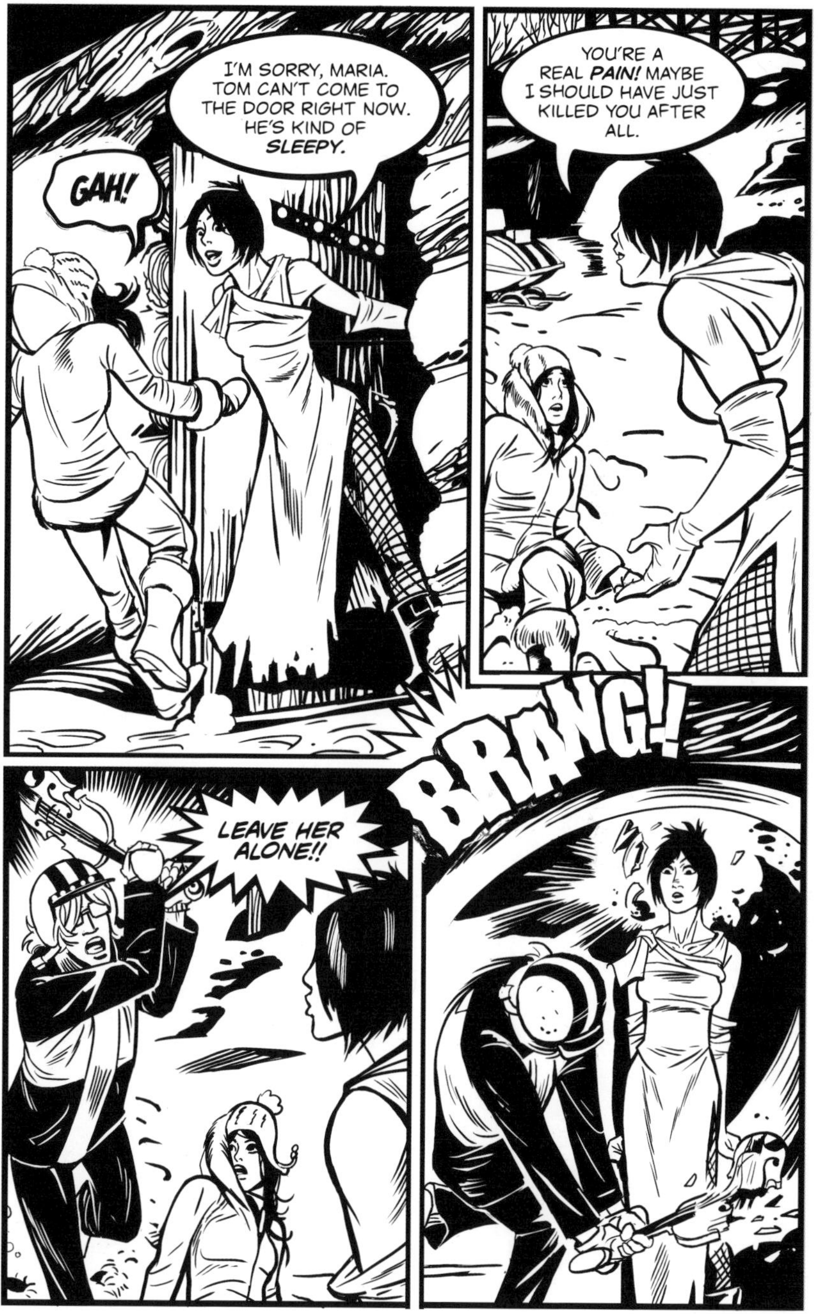
I'M SORRY, MARIA. TOM CAN'T COME TO THE DOOR RIGHT NOW. HE'S KIND OF SLEEPY.
GAH!
YOU'RE A REAL PAIN! MAYBE I SHOULD HAVE JUST KILLED YOU AFTER ALL.
LEAVE HER ALONE!!
BRANG!!

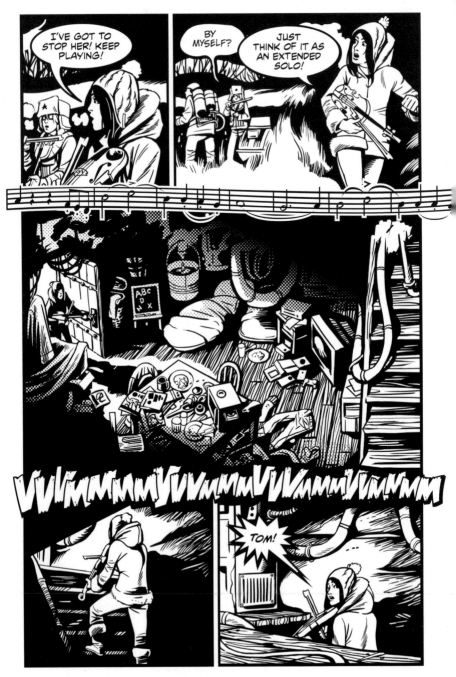

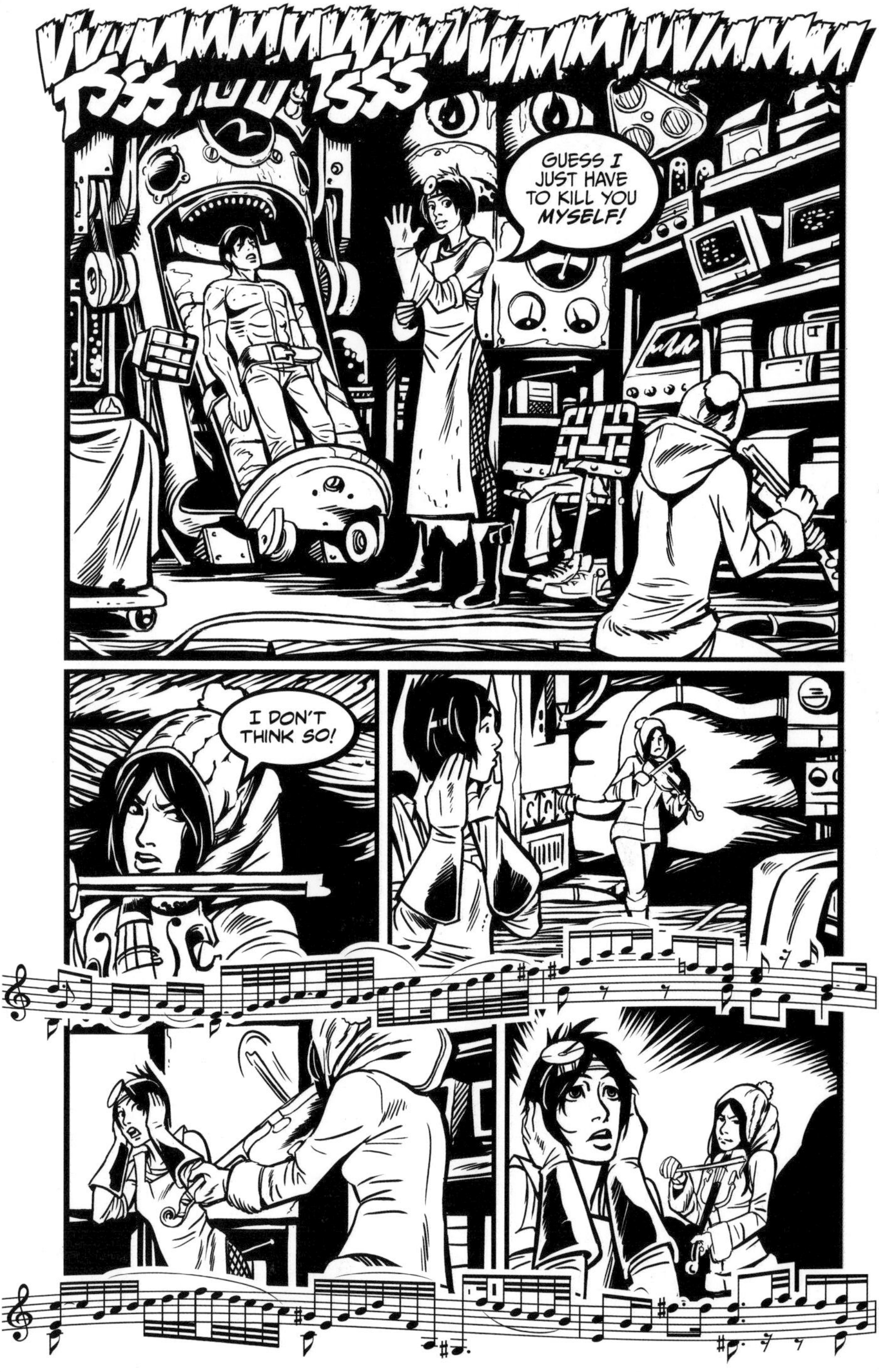
VVVMMMMVVVMMVVVMMMVVVMMMM
TSSS TUU TSSS
GUESS I JUST HAVE TO KILL YOU MYSELF!
I DON'T THINK SO!

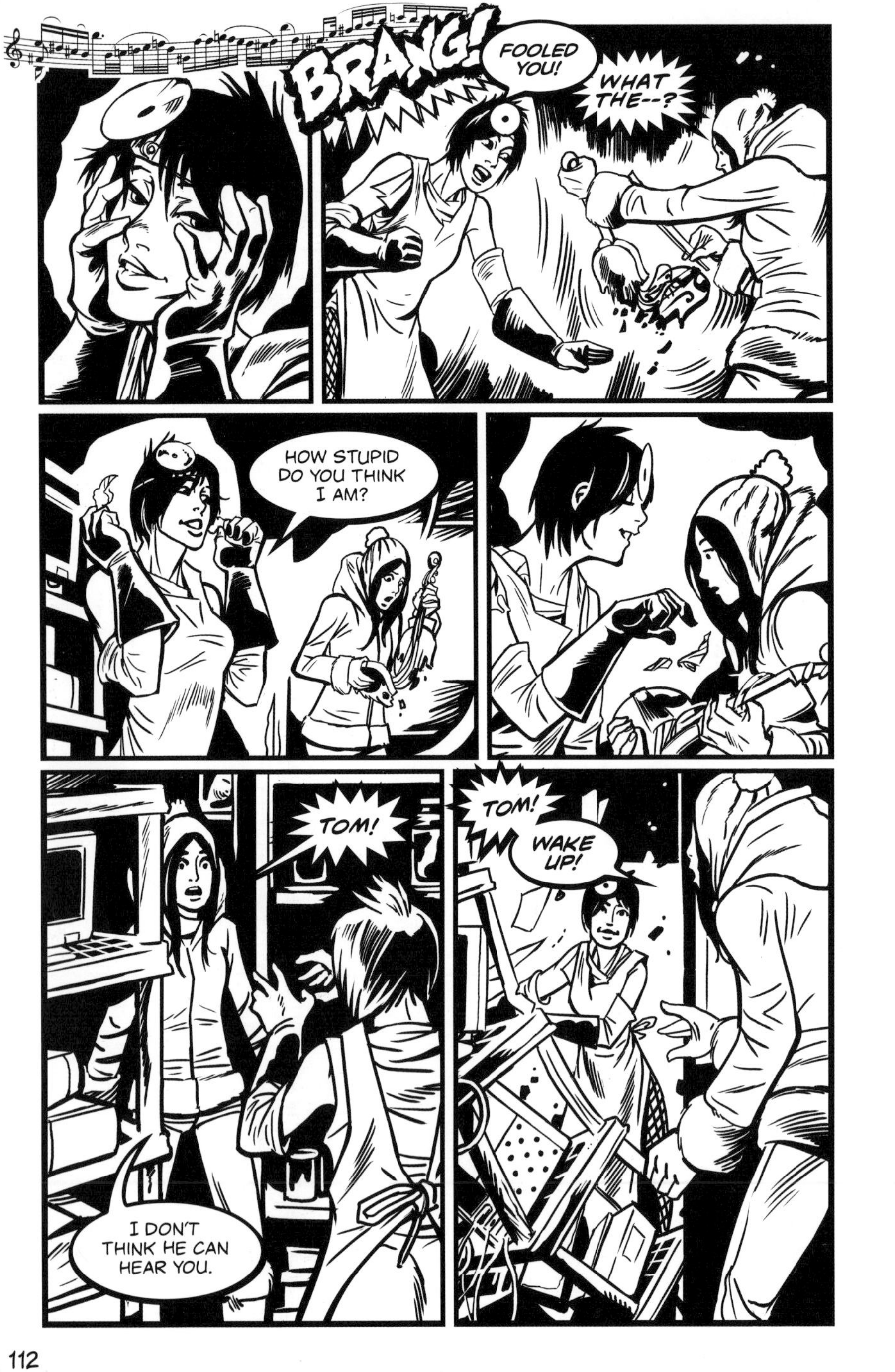
BRANG!
FOOLED YOU!
WHAT THE--?
HOW STUPID DO YOU THINK I AM?
TOM!
TOM!
WAKE UP!
I DON'T THINK HE CAN HEAR YOU.

113

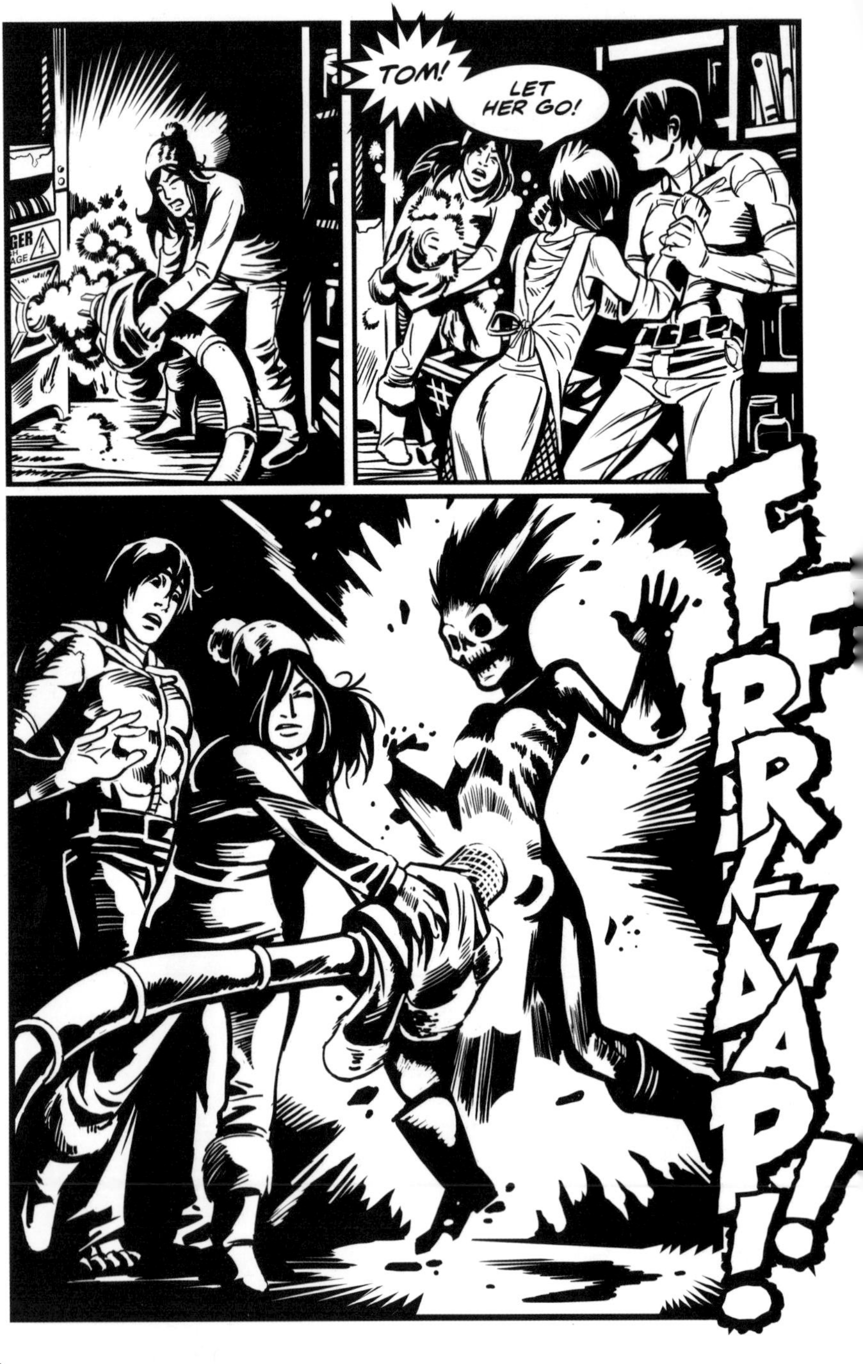
TOM!
LET HER GO!
FRZZDAP!!

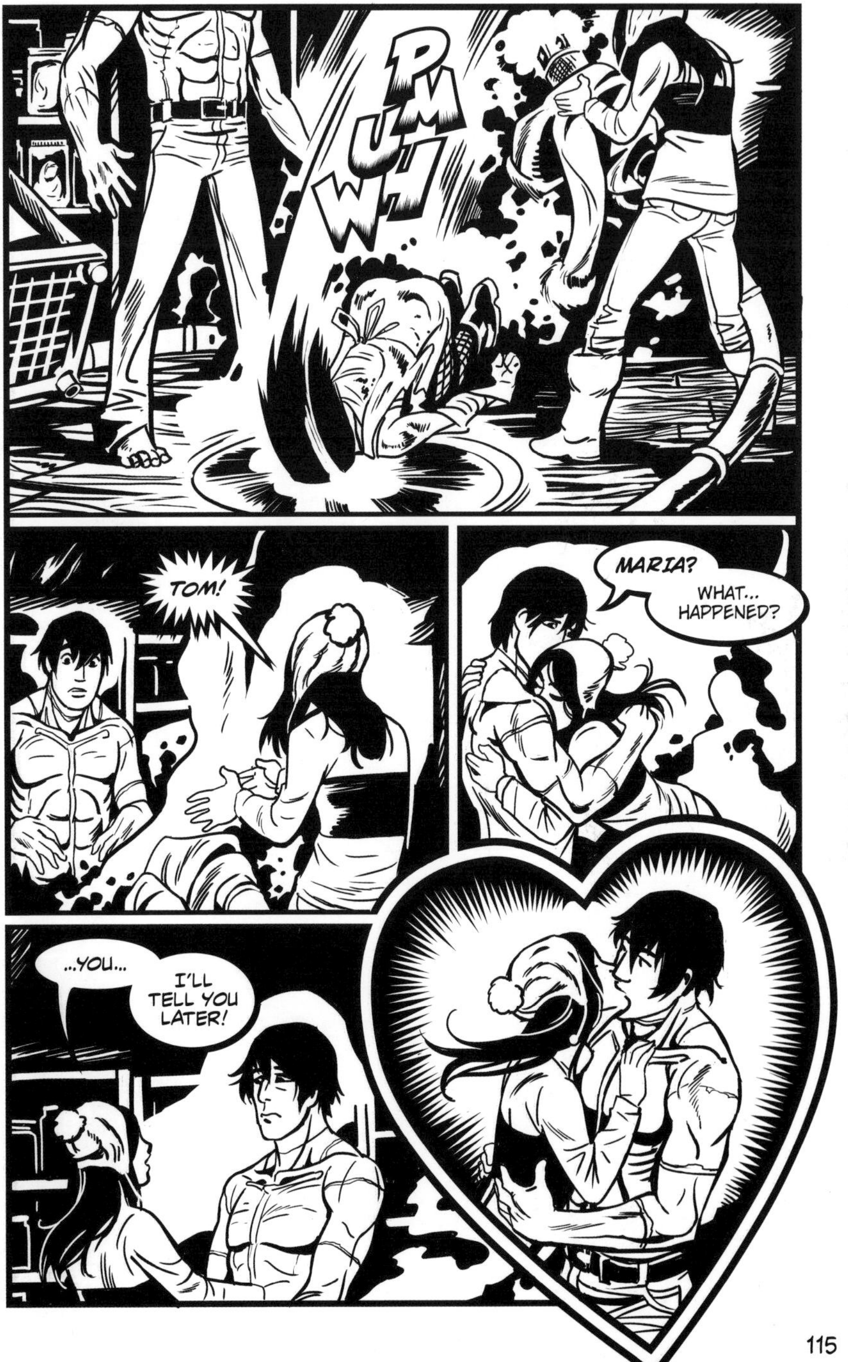
WHUMP
TOM!
MARIA?
WHAT... HAPPENED?
...YOU...
I'LL TELL YOU LATER!

119

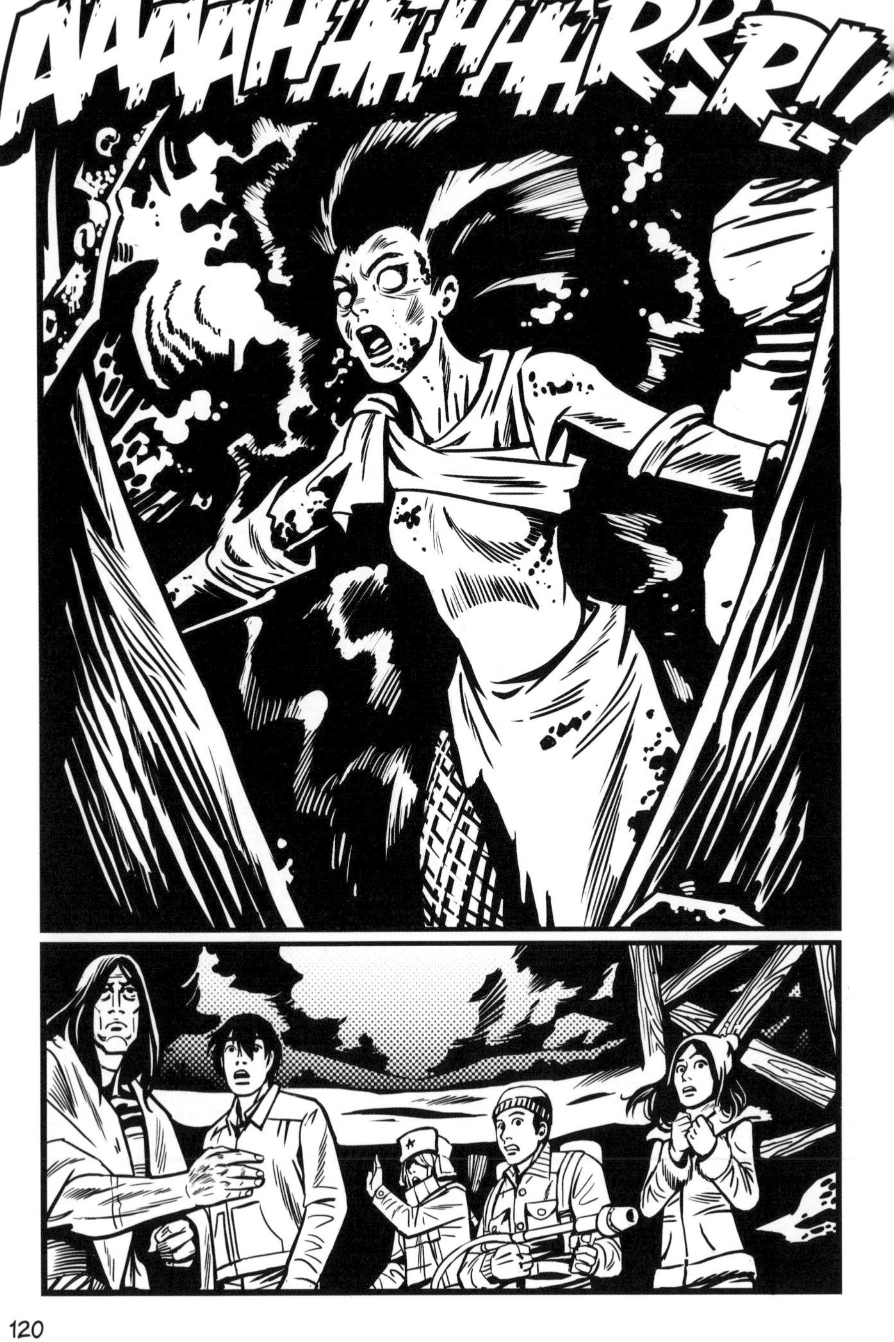
AAAAHHHHHHHRRR!!

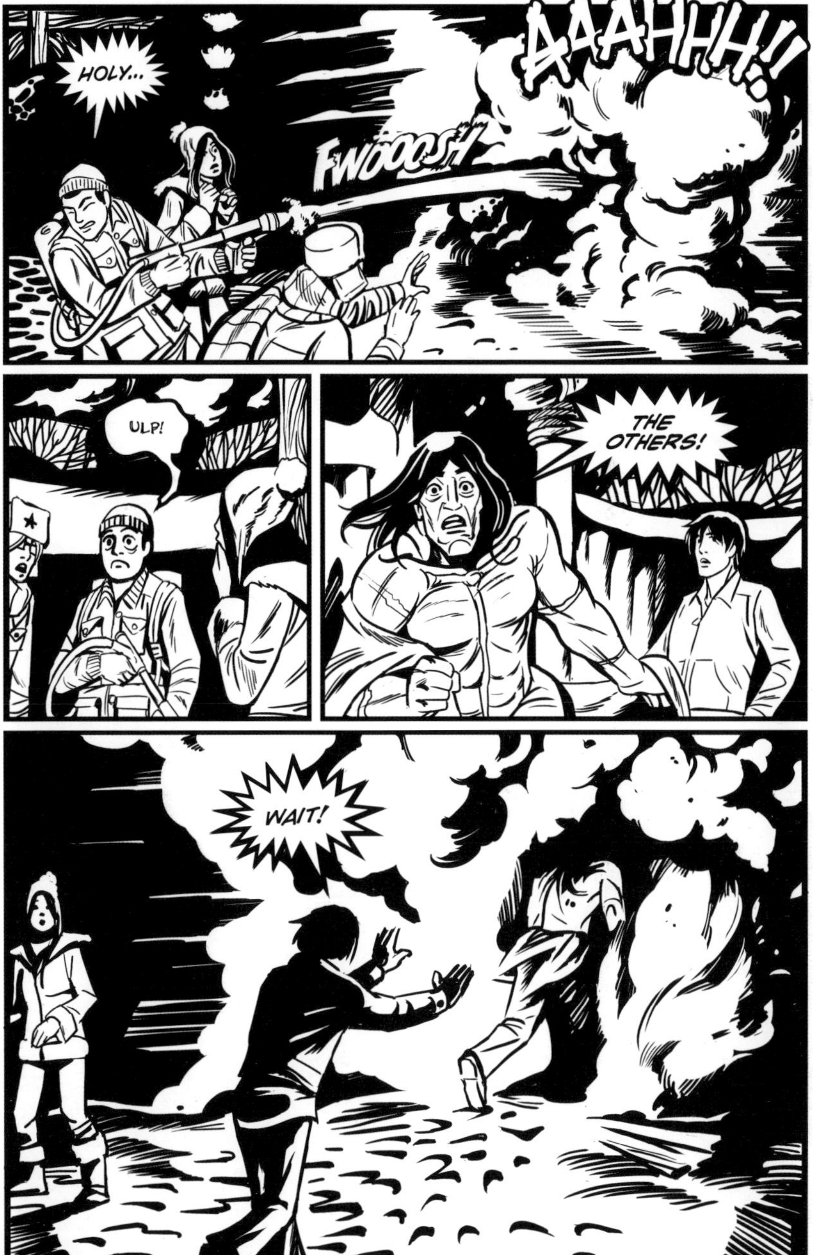
HOLY...
FWOOOSH
AAAHHH!!
ULP!
THE OTHERS!
WAIT!

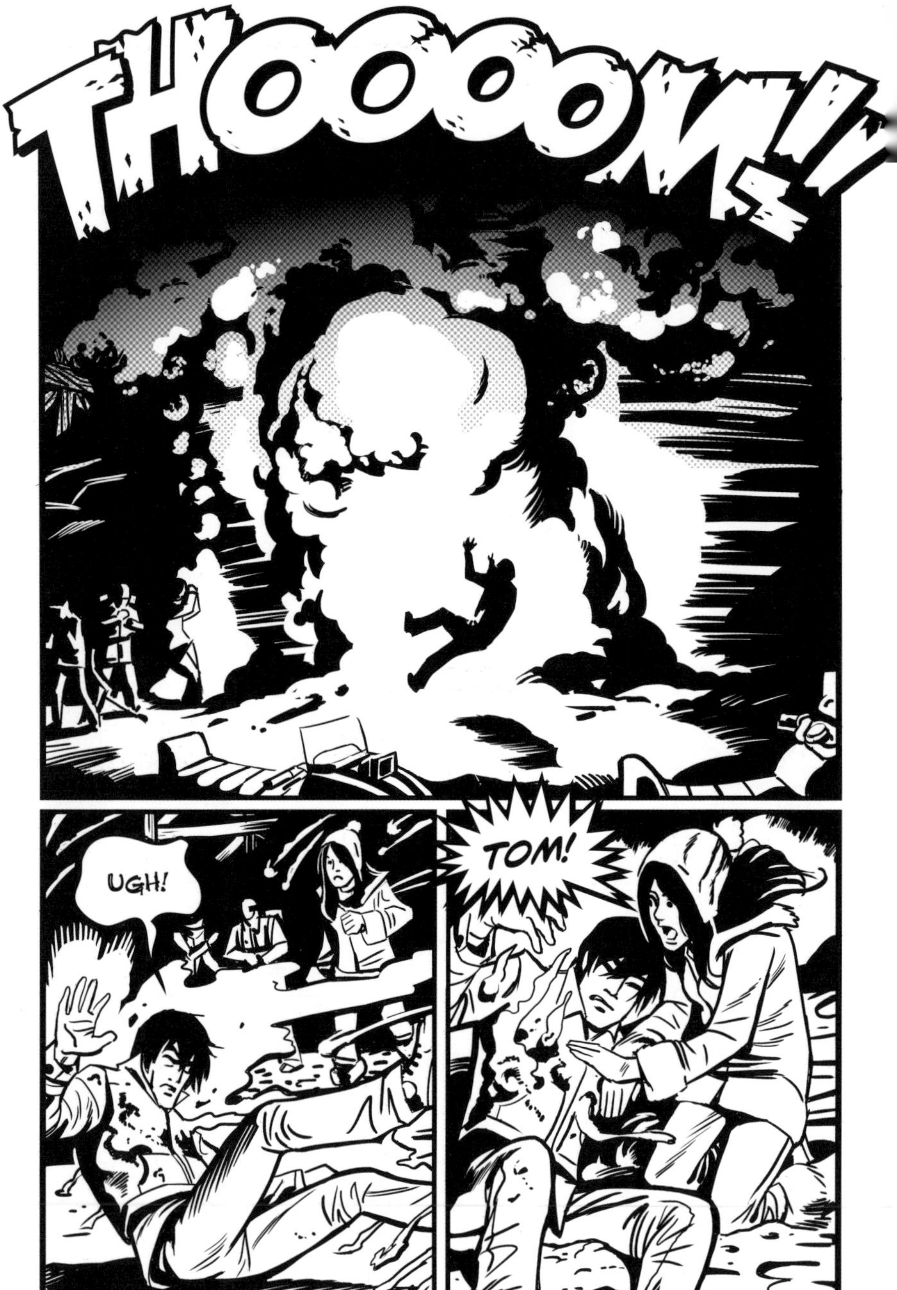
THOOOOM!!
UGH!
TOM!

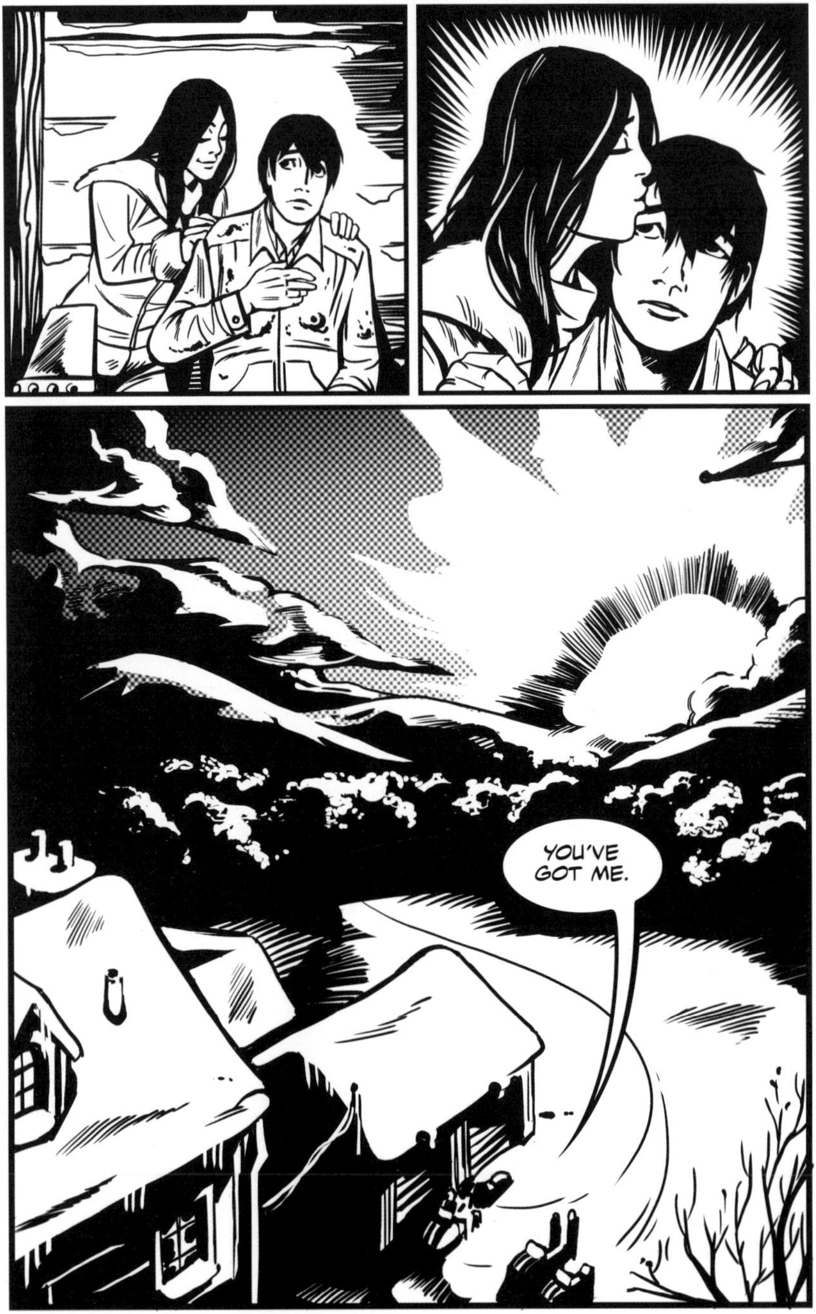
YOU'VE GOT ME.

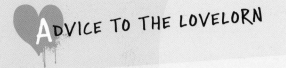

ADVICE TO THE LOVELORN

ELSA C. WRITES:

When you date a Frankenstein, do you have to be careful not to accidentally pop some stitches?

MARIA REPLIES:

Not anymore, Elsa. But good question. In the old days, surgical techniques and medical supplies weren't as good as they are now. Back then, if you held hands with a Frankenstein, you had to worry about ending up holding just a hand. Today, you can be confident that parts are going to stay put!

JENNIFER B. WRITES:

Why would you want to date a Frankenstein? Aren't they all ugly?

MARIA REPLIES:

You'd be surprised! Anyway, who says that it's all about looks? A great-looking guy might be a really ugly person on the inside. And sometimes the more you get to know someone really special, the more attractive they are to you. Sounds hard to believe, but it's true!

MARY S. WRITES:

Frankenstein is the name of the scientist, not the monster. Why do people always get that wrong? It makes me crazy!

MARIA REPLIES:

Not really a question about dating, Mary, but it's true—that's a common error. In the original novel, *Frankenstein, or The Modern Prometheus*, the monster doesn't have any name at all. But soon after, people started calling him Frankenstein. I guess it's because Frankenstein is a lot easier to say than Frankenstein's monster. Maybe the author should have given the monster a catchy name.

ABOUT THE AUTHOR
AND THE ARTIST

PAUL STORRIE was born and raised in Detroit, Michigan. He has returned to live there again and again after living in other cities and states. He began writing professionally in 1998 and has written comics for Caliber Comics, Moonstone Books, Marvel Comics, and DC Comics. His titles for Graphic Universe™ include *Hercules, Robin Hood, Yu the Great,* and *Amaterasu.* Other titles he has worked on include *Robyn of Sherwood* (featuring stories about Robin Hood's daughter), *Batman Beyond, Gotham Girls, Captain America: Red, White and Blue, Mutant X,* and *Revisionary.*

Creator of the webcomic *Astray3* at www.astray3.com, ELDON COWGUR is a seeker of action and adventure. Whether he finds it through the point of a pencil or far afield, where there is derring-do to be done he is there. Most times, he can be found at his humble northwest Arkansas dwelling, drawing wild tales of curious locations with his roguish pet conure Quetzal. When at leisure, he may be found enjoying the outdoors or studying the art of comics. Eldon is also very fond of robots.